LINDA CONRAD

When asked about her favorite things, Linda Conrad lists a longtime love affair with her husband, her sweetheart of a dog named KiKi and a sunny afternoon with nothing to do but read a good book. Inspired by generations of storytellers in her family and pleased to have many happy readers' comments, Linda continues creating her own sensuous and suspenseful stories about compelling characters finding love.

A bestselling author of more than twenty-five books, Linda has received numerous industry awards, among them a National Reader's Choice Award, a Maggie, a Write Touch Readers' Award and an *RT Book Reviews* Reviewers' Choice Award. To contact Linda, read more about her books or to sign up for her newsletter and/or contests, go to her website at www.lindaconrad.com.

LORETH ANNE WHITE

Loreth Anne White was born and raised in southern Africa, but now lives in Whistler, a ski resort in the moody British Columbian Coast Mountain range. It's a place of vast wilderness, larger-than-life characters, epic adventure and romance—the perfect place to escape reality. It's no wonder she was inspired to abandon a sixteen-year career as a journalist to escape into a world of romance fiction filled with dangerous men and adventurous women.

When she's not writing you will find her long-distance running, biking or skiing on the trails and generally trying to avoid the bears—albeit not very successfully. She calls this work, because it's when the best ideas come. For a peek into her world, visit her website, www.lorethannewhite.com. She'd love to hear from you.

LINDA CONRAD

LORETH ANNE WHITE

Desert Knights

ROMANTIC

SUSPENSE

ISBN-13: 978-0-373-27731-5

DESERT KNIGHTS

Copyright © 2011 by Harlequin Books S.A.

Recycling programs for this product may not exist in your area.

The publisher acknowledges the copyright holders of the individual works as follows:

BODYGUARD SHEIK
Copyright © 2011 by Linda Lucas Sankpill

SHEIK'S CAPTIVE
Copyright © 2011 by Loreth Beswetherick

This edition published by arrangement with Harlequin Books S.A.

For questions and comments about the quality of this book please contact us at Customer_eCare@Harlequin.ca.

® and TM are trademarks of Harlequin Books S.A., used under license. Trademarks indicated with ® are registered in the United States Patent and Trademark Office, the Canadian Trade Marks Office and in other countries.

www.Harlequin.com

Printed in U.S.A.

CONTENTS

BODYGUARD SHEIK   7
Linda Conrad

SHEIK'S CAPTIVE   115
Loreth Anne White

Dear Reader,

Just in time for summer, we have four high-octane reads from Harlequin Romantic Suspense! Reader favorite Justine Davis writes romance with a twist in *Enemy Waters* (#1659), a searing tale of a woman in hiding, whose heart is aroused by the man hired to find her. No one does passion like Merline Lovelace, and you'll love her next Code Name: Danger story, *Strangers When We Meet* (#1660), which features two agents from different worlds, potentially on opposite sides of an investigation. You won't want to miss this sexy roller-coaster ride!

Two beloved authors, Linda Conrad and Loreth Anne White, bring you two sheik stories designed to get your pulse racing. In *Desert Knights* (#1661), you'll meet two heroes and two heroines facing danger in the desert. To round out this already exciting month, fabulous Harlequin Nocturne and Romantic Suspense author Karen Whiddon delivers *The CEO's Secret Baby* (#1662), where a handsome hero thought dead returns…and makes a startling discovery!

This month is all about finding love against the odds and those adventures lurking around every corner. So as you lounge on the beach or in your favorite chair, lose yourself in one of these gems from Harlequin Romantic Suspense!

Sincerely,

Patience Bloom

Senior Editor

BODYGUARD SHEIK

Linda Conrad

To Amy Moore Benson.
Thanks for making it happen!

And to a dear friend, Loreth Anne White,
for giving a crazy idea a shot.

You two are the best!

Dateline: Kandahár, Afghanistan

Three senior Taliban members were shot and killed while eating lunch at a crowded outdoor market in the western section of the city today. No group has taken credit for the precisely executed attack. No bystanders were injured and no one claims to have seen the killer.

Unnamed sources at the Pentagon say all three shots were fired from the same weapon at a distance of over four hundred yards, an amazing feat of marksmanship. The CIA has refused comment.

—AP

Chapter 1

Death, in all its facets, troubled Morgan Bell's mind as she rode to her destiny in the back of a Sikorsky helicopter.

For over half her adult life she'd concentrated her talents on killing. She was good at what she did. An expert, they said.

But what kind of life did that make? It hadn't been enough for her to train as an expert marksman, one of the best in the world. No, sir, not good enough for rough and tough Morgan Bell. Her record 725-yard rifle shots no longer won awards in contests. She hadn't competed in nearly a decade. Over the last ten years, all her carefully contrived shots took out killers and madmen, not paper targets.

When said in a forthright tone of voice, even in her head, those words sounded almost righteous. Pure at heart.

In her mind and soul, though, Morgan knew she was no better than the butchers and murderers that her superiors sent her to dispatch. And that wasn't who she wanted to be anymore.

Running without lights no more than twenty feet off the desert sands, the copter pilot darted his craft in and out of blind canyons, staying in the moon's shadows. Morgan's fingers clung to her rifle case with a viselike grip as she studied the expert flyer through her NVGs, glowing eerily green against the black, night sky.

Suddenly struck with a bout of depression, caused by both the stark landscape out the open door at her side and by the thought of why she'd volunteered to be on this mission in the first place, Morgan trained her gaze on the men riding in the seats next to hers. Dark, brooding men, all of them. She'd spent the last three weeks in training with them. But now, the mere sight of the deadly determination in their postures was enough to give her a start.

She felt determined, too. The situation demanded it. But she couldn't help wondering how she had allowed her life to deteriorate into nothing more than a series of determined and dire situations like this one.

Morgan was almost finished with this kind of life. She'd recently taken early retirement from the CIA, and was ready to head back to her family's Wyoming ranch to find a new life. A different life. A decent life with people who cared, like the one she'd had as a girl.

Yet, as a favor to an old friend, here she was, taking a detour and flying to one last mission. A last mission with deadly consequences and grim implications.

Her headset clicked on. "Get set," the pilot informed the team. "Our target zone is about to be hit by a weather event. I won't be able to set it down. You'll have to unload on the fly."

Morgan didn't like unplanned events on a mission. A sniper must plan every last detail, right down to the wind direction. Nothing could ever be left to chance. Too tricky to go barging right into enemy territory without working out the thousands of calculations necessary for a successful shot. Any number of things could go wrong without flawless plans.

She turned her gaze to the open doorway beside her seat and drew in a harsh breath. Where there had been moonlight and rock cliffs zooming past only moments ago, now a ground-to-sky, dense fog loomed in its place. Slinging the straps for her pack and rifle case over her head, she tensed in her seat, ready to abort the mission.

"What…?" Morgan didn't manage to get the question out of her mouth.

"Sandstorm! Go!" The pilot fought to steady his copter, hovering it over a tiny stretch of clear ground.

From the seat behind her, one of the team members reached out and grabbed her arm. "I'll go first. You're next. I'll act as your descent partner."

Petrified, she said nothing. Just stared at him as though he were speaking a foreign language.

"Never mind," he yelled, trying to be heard over the sound of the rotors.

He tightened his grip on her arm with one hand and snaked the other around her waist. "We go together."

The next thing she knew, Morgan was flying. Out the copter door, heading toward the dark ground somewhere in the hazy distance below.

"Bend your knees and roll!"

The quick rush of adrenaline as he hit the ground nearly caused Karim Kadir to forget his assignment. His one, clear and all-encompassing responsibility on this, his first, mission: the *sniper's* welfare.

But forgetting could never happen. Not with this woman. She was unforgettable.

Scrambling around on all fours, he swallowed down the exhilaration of the jump and located her in the swirling dust kicked up by the rotors' wash. The sniper was lying flat on the ground but still breathing heavily.

Despite the whining engine noise and the blasting winds, Karim thought he heard words coming through his headset. "Abort! Abort!"

Though he pushed at the earpiece, trying to make the transmission clearer, the copter pilot's voice grew faint in the static. Every sound, every word, broke up and Karim could see nothing through the sudden tornado of winds and dust surrounding them.

It didn't matter. His duty was clear. He found Morgan's inert body again and quickly checked over her arms and legs for any breaks.

"Take your hands off me, you muscle-bound fathead," she shouted through gritted teeth. "What the hell is the matter with you?" Batting at his arms, she scooted back out of reach.

"We need to move. Find cover from the sandstorm."

"Bite me. I'm not going anywhere with you. I'm waiting right here until the pilot comes back for us. Didn't you hear him abort?"

At least she was uninjured. But Karim did not have time to argue.

He grabbed her up and got in her face. "Retrieve your equipment." Without waiting for her move, he bent and pulled her rifle case up with his free hand. "The copter won't be back until the storm lets up. We need to take cover *now*."

She squirmed a little, but as he dragged her across the sand she kept silent and at last started moving with him instead of against him. Probably she'd closed her mouth to avoid having sand fill it. The sandstorm had hit in earnest.

Karim didn't care why she was cooperating. He was just glad he didn't have to carry her, her forty-pound pack and her rifle case, in addition to his own sixty-pound pack, in what must be thirty-miles-an-hour winds.

He backed them up to an uneven rock formation. This was as good of a shelter as he was likely to find, considering he couldn't see two feet in front of his face.

"Remember your training," he urged, whispering loudly in her ear as he released her.

She shot him an anger-filled glance. Then, ripping her rifle case from his hands, she cradled the case in the crook of her arm and turned her back. Inching her nose as close to the rough limestone wall of rock as she possibly could, she covered her face with her hands. Karim stepped in behind her back. Finding he was unable to totally cover her body with his own, he reached out and pulled the backpack straps down her shoulders.

"Hey!"

"Take the pack off."

She complied with a small grimace and then swung back into position as she had been instructed in class. Karim snugged his chest against her back and braced his hands flat on the wall at either side of her body. He prayed his own pack would offer some protection for both of them from the driving sand. Already the backs of his hands were stinging and he'd had to bow his head to keep taking breaths of air.

A hell of a way to begin his first mission.

The roar of the storm still rang in her ears, but Morgan was fairly certain the worst had passed them by. She wasn't having to brace her body against the pounding winds anymore.

At that moment, Karim relaxed his body, too, and stomped away, pulling his feet out of ten inches of built-up sand as he went. She jerked her feet up as well and then swung around to give him a piece of her mind. Before she could say anything, he scrubbed his hands across his eyes, trying to remove the grit. Seeing him work so hard to focus on her face made her hold her tongue. The skin on his chin looked raw, and the beet-red color of the backs of his hands stopped her cold.

For three weeks they'd been training side by side, but they didn't know much about each other. There had been no time for relationship-building while learning desert survival and memorizing the topography of the area. But she'd had plenty of time to notice his strong jawline. The way his black-as-midnight hair curled just so against his neck. How his strong, masculine hands could suddenly turn gentle as he taught her rope-tying.

Swallowing past her parched throat, she blinked away the inappropriate thoughts.

The entire rescue team had dressed in bedouin male attire for the mission, complete with heavy scarves as head coverings. Without them, she was sure Karim's scalp would've been sandblasted and bleeding by now.

"Are you okay?" It wasn't what she'd planned for the last hour to say to him, but seeing his condition changed all that.

As he managed to clear his eyes, he grumbled, "That's my question for you. I'm still the bodyguard on this mission."

A flare of anger at both his impulsive actions and those controlling words competed in her mind with the sympathy she thought she'd been feeling for his pain. And both of those emotions, the anger and the sympathy, did nothing to cover a far deeper, more sensual shudder she'd been feeling low in the belly every time he'd glanced in her direction.

Not like her. Such distractions were not her style.

"This mission is aborted," she ground out. How many times would she be required to say it? "You must've heard the pilot."

He grinned at her, using the same careless grin that made her stomach do somersaults. "I believe I heard the pilot say the *landing* was aborted. Not the mission."

She waved her hand at his face, trying to make him see the truth. "A sandstorm is too huge a change in plans. We cannot continue from here."

Remembering her rifle, she stopped arguing long enough to dust off the cover and check it out. Her rifle was her life, her third arm. Nothing could happen to harm it.

"The timing will be off now." Once reassured about her weapon, she fought again to make him understand. "Changes in wind direction. A dozen other details. The mission must be scrubbed. When do you think the copter can come back for us?"

Morgan was having trouble concentrating on what she was saying while he stood still and watched her pace. She realized her inopportune infatuation with this swarthy, unpredictable man could rob her of her discipline. Maintaining control was the one thing that had kept her going for most of her adult life. Control gave her the strength to carry on after the worst of times. She could not afford to lose it now.

That look in his dark eyes seemed…she wasn't sure what. Maybe disappointed?

"Aborting the mission is not your call. Let's clean up a little, drink some water and try to raise command on the SAT phone. Okay?"

Sounded sensible. Which would be in total opposition to what she knew so far about Karim's personality. An adrenaline junkie and impulsive as hell. The man was her worst nightmare.

"Fine." It took her a moment to locate her pack, covered by about a foot of fine-grained sand. "It may be months before I get all the sand out of everything."

Every crevice in her body felt gritty. A shower suddenly sounded like the best plan yet.

Karim handed her his high-tech water bladder. "Take a few sips to clear your throat."

After she drank her fill, Morgan handed the container back. As he lifted it to his lips, she noted that he sneaked careful glances at her out of fathomless ebony eyes. Rattled by his unceasing perusal, her own gaze landed on his lips as they touched the same rim that had just touched hers. He swallowed, then ran his tongue over his bottom lip as though he knew what she was thinking. A spark ignited in her gut and sizzled along her spine.

Dear God, what was the matter with her? Turning her back, she bent to dust off her pants. No thoughts at all would be better than thoughts of kissing a man like Karim.

Remembering the strong, sand-filled winds, she reached up to feel around the edges of her head scarf. She would need to make sure her hair was all tucked up under the scarf before they went anywhere. Not that she thought she would be needing her disguise for much longer. The copter would be back for them at any moment.

Before they'd come on this mission, it had been the consensus of opinion that in a backward place like Zabbarán, she would need to disguise herself as a bedouin man in order to avoid confrontations with any of the locals. That idea had been fine by her.

Morgan did not do up-close-and-personal confrontations. Not with anyone. All her deadly confrontations over the last twelve years had happened at a distance of four hundred yards—plus.

She turned back to Karim in time to see him trying to get a signal on his satellite phone. "Nothing. Must still be interference from the sandstorm."

Well, that sucked. "How long do you think it will be until we can reach them?"

"Maybe a long time. Too long to stick around here. When the sun breaks fully over the mountains, we'll be too exposed. Both to the elements and to any passing Taj Zabbar patrols."

It had taken her a while to get the names of the players straight for this wild and crazy drama her ex-CIA partner had talked her into. The Taj Zabbar would be the bad guys, she knew that much. Really bad from the sounds of things. Apparently they hated everybody, but especially the Kadir family.

Tarik Kadir, her partner on several interagency task force operations while she was with the CIA, had been the one who'd asked for her help. She owed Tarik. He'd saved her life on more than one occasion.

So without much of an argument to the contrary, she'd *volunteered* to work with the Kadir family inside an uncivilized desert country. And already this mission had turned into a royal screwup.

She figured she would be sorry she'd asked this, but… "What do you propose?"

"The original plan called for us to head over those mountains." Karim pinned her with a sincere look. "I say we stick with the plan. Start out. Maybe we'll be able to catch a SAT signal nearer the mountain's crest."

"You aren't considering going ahead with the mission if the others can't meet up with us."

He didn't answer her non-question right away, but the look in his eyes shouted loud enough.

"You can't be considering *not* going ahead with the mission." He finally made himself clear using a twist on her own words. "Not with what's at stake."

Morgan didn't wish to think about *the stakes.* Her missions had always consisted of planning the strike and executing the strike. Plain and simple. Complicated issues like politics and terrorism, even life and death, could never be considerations in her world. Such complications might interfere with her concentration.

However, this time Karim would not let her shift her focus away from their true goal. "You understand there's an innocent child's life at stake, Morgan? A little two-year-old boy by the name of Matin whose parents were murdered in front of his eyes. He's living a life under a death sentence and will die if we can't reach him in time."

A huge, gripping ache in her chest left her nauseated and dizzy. She hadn't wanted to consider the "victim." Only the target. But she drew in several deep breaths and tried to block the distraction.

Still, even with her renowned mental discipline, could she possibly concentrate on a mission where a child's life hung in the balance? What if all their efforts weren't enough?

"Well, are you with me or not?" Karim held out his hand.

Straightening her shoulders, she drew herself up into a rigid line and took his hand. "I'm with you. We'll stick to the plan."

It would have to be good enough. *She* would have to be good enough.

Chapter 2

A little later Karim reached out his hand and grabbed Morgan's forearm, dragging her up the last five feet of steep trail. Then he let her sidestep around him and take the lead again.

They'd been making good progress up the slope. Half the time he followed her to be sure she didn't slip. The rest of the time he led, urging her to keep up with the pace he set.

As the sun rose higher in the crystal-blue sky, he decided it was time for a rest period. It hadn't taken the desert sun long to begin bubbling off boulders and small rocks along their makeshift path. Heat, throbbing and humming, rippled across stark sandstone spires as the sweat began trickling down his neck.

But look at her. Calm. Cool. Like ice water must run in her veins.

He found himself admiring her as he would a complicated piece of machinery. For most of his life, his world had revolved around perfectly attuned electrical or mechanical components: connectors, sockets, integrated circuits, user interfaces and motherboards. Elegant design had always intrigued him.

This mission was a first attempt at turning his life around. To give in to his long-standing desire to awaken every morning in the real world instead of a world full of avatars and algorithms. He needed to feel a positive existence pulsating through his bloodstream for a change. To be really alive.

And to mean something. To fight the good fight with his family and avenge his father's death.

She meant something. People counted on her to do her job with no fuss, and she didn't let them down.

As she took the next tenuous step up an old, pebbled, mountain goat's trail, her sandaled feet slipped out from under her and she reached forward, trying to grasp any protruding handhold in the stone. He didn't stop for a consideration of the sweetness of her backside or the fact that his palms were now firmly planted against those material-covered cheeks. He just kept her from sliding backward.

Later, he might need to take a few deep breaths. But for right now, he jumped up beside her on the trail and gathered her into his arms, balancing them together in the small space.

"You're okay."

She glared at him. "I am. Now release me."

When he drew his arms back, she turned and practically pole-vaulted the next few feet around a switchback. He stayed with her, as close as he dared, determined to be the best possible bodyguard.

"Let's take a break," he said as they rounded a granite outcropping and came upon an overhanging ledge that would provide shelter from the sun.

Without saying a word, she ducked into the shade and perched her bottom on a flat rock. Shrugging out of her pack, she worked her shoulders, as if every millimeter of muscle ached. His shoulders were plenty stiff, too, but that couldn't matter. He dropped his pack and squatted down on his heels.

"You need to rehydrate." Using the quick release on his chest strap, he removed one of the bladders of his CamelBak hydration system and handed it to her. "It wouldn't hurt us to take in salt and protein at this point, either."

He felt another bead of sweat appear on his forehead and shoved his head scarf back out of the way. Morgan looked askance, disapproving of his bare head, but then ignored him as she raised the bladder to her lips and drank.

She didn't need to remove her scarf for him to remember the heavy mass of chestnut hair she'd twisted into a prim knot underneath. That hair had become a vivid feature starring in all his dreams for the last few weeks. Sleek. Silky. An image of those satin strands trailing across his belly as she leaned over his chest rudely interrupted his thoughts at inopportune times, as though he'd accidently come across a porno ad on the web.

"You're an idiot," he murmured under his breath.

She could never know what he'd been thinking—dreaming. He wanted this mission to go right. For more than one reason. And it would never be right if she knew he'd been lusting for her since the day they'd met.

Digging around in his pack, he found the Nitro-Tech high-protein bars. "Here you go. Sodium and high protein in one almost enjoyable package."

"Hmm." She gave him a wry look but took the bar he offered. "You going to try phoning *home* again?"

He needed her on his side. It was more than a possibility that they would have to accomplish this mission without backup.

"In a moment." He took a drink and unwrapped a bar of

his own. "You know," he began by way of making small talk. "I've been watching you. You move quietly. Like a panther. Excellent moves."

"What you mean is I move quietly. Like a panther— *considering* I'm a woman."

Shaken by her words, Karim swallowed the tasteless protein bar, wondering if they were true. He hadn't spent a lot of time around women and definitely no time around a woman as strong, skilled and determined as this one. Still, he didn't believe he was prejudiced either for or against women in general.

"No," he offered after a moment. "I don't mean that. I mean, I respect your abilities and I'm impressed with how you make the best out of trying circumstances."

"I expected this mission to be difficult." She eyed him carefully. "Three days across the desert in an inhospitable land is not like a walk on the beach.

"What I didn't expect was to be hustled out of the helicopter in the middle of a sandstorm and end up with only one other person on my team."

She'd said the last as though she didn't believe he could handle the job by himself. But he could. He knew his capabilities as surely as he knew the sun would set behind the mountains in a few hours. She had no way of knowing that, of course. So he'd cut her some slack.

"I'll try the phone again." He rose, moved out of the shade and into the sun in order to get a clearer signal from the satellite.

The woman fascinated him. Good thing, because they would be spending a lot of time together over the next seventy-two hours. He had a feeling she was just as curious about him, though he wasn't positive they were in sync over the type of curiosity they each felt. For sure, they would have to work hard at overcoming their differences and becoming comrades in arms.

And he would have to work a lot harder at setting aside his lustful desires long enough to accomplish the mission.

Morgan slowly chewed her protein bar and watched while Karim captured a satellite signal and spoke into the phone. From what she could ascertain by his side of the conversation, the two of them would be on their own for most of the mission.

Now that she'd made the decision to continue, she would need to find a way to make the best of things. Somehow, she would have to forge a working relationship, perhaps even a sort of field friendship, with the man. It would be tricky, becoming his friend when she still felt a sensual chill at his every glance. But she was a professional. She imagined she could even handle a little desert flirtation, if it came down to that. Not that she ever had in the past. But this mission was proving to be quite different from the others.

He hung up and swung back under their rock ledge and into the shade. "Good news and bad."

Time for her to get on with what she needed to do.

"I gathered as much. Do we have a new plan? New time-table?"

His deep eyes quietly studied hers quietly for a moment. "They're working on the timetable. It seems this section of desert is suddenly swarming with Taj Zabbar patrols. But headquarters doesn't believe their radar tagged our copter entering their territory. The sandstorm apparently covered our flight trajectory better than we could've hoped. And from satellite photos, it also didn't look to Tarik as if the enemy troops were seeking out a commando raiding party. Their movements aren't in a search grid. Like they don't know we're in the territory."

"So we continue?"

"Tarik is working to get through to some of his covert agents in Zabbarán to find out what's going on. Meanwhile we're supposed to keep up with the plan as long as we can, but we're to check in tomorrow night, if we can get a signal."

He waited, as though holding his breath and hoping she wouldn't make a stink over the change. It was plain to see the time had come for her to make her first big attempt at having a friendship.

She nodded once and reached for her pack. "We're about to hit the twenty-minute mark on this stop. Time to move."

Desert survival training taught them that successful rest periods lasted more than five minutes, but any more than twenty minutes usually meant stiff muscles on the next leg. They had a long way to go before a planned sleep period. She would have to forge their budding friendship along the trail.

"Well…" He blinked a couple of times and then set to work, tightening his own pack. "Yes. And it's midmorning, too. Time for the sunglasses."

He tossed her a pair of high-tech glasses with special nonglare lenses. The CIA had designed them for fieldwork in Afghanistan. They cut the glare for the wearer and ensured no enemy would spot sunlight bouncing off them in the mountain passes.

During their survival training, she'd noticed Karim's biggest interest seemed to lay with the technological innovations. Perhaps that would give her a place to begin.

As they started up the trail, she dug into the pocket of the rifle case and came up with her laser triangulation GPS. She'd programmed the maps and their route in before the team started out. The handheld device was specifically designed for her use in the field. No one else in the world had one of these babies yet.

"Looks like we're only one hundred and twenty-three yards

from the summit." Without letting him know, she checked his expression and found she'd been right. His eyes were glued to the device in her palm. Men and their toys. "Unless there's an obstruction in the path, we'll be at the top in record time."

"Nice piece of equipment."

"What, you mean this?" She handed it over. "It's a prototype. But I understand it will shortly be in use by the military. Do you need a quick tutorial?"

"No, but thanks." He beamed all over as he punched a couple of buttons. "Very nice."

Wasn't it interesting that a man with more bulging muscles than a human had a right to possess could understand the intricacies of a highly technical piece of equipment at first glance? Who was he, really?

The trail widened out enough to allow them to walk side by side. "Since we're going to be spending so much time together, maybe we should learn a little bit about each other's backgrounds. You probably know more than I would wish about me, but I don't know anything about you, yet. Wanna start?"

Karim handed the handheld device back, wondering whether it was a good idea for the two of them to get to know each other better. He'd been daydreaming about getting to know her—intimately, not as the comrade on a life-and-death mission.

So yeah, he'd like to know her a whole lot better in one way, but could he settle for finding out what made her tick?

Before he had the chance to learn anything, he supposed he would have to open up about his own life first. "Well, I'm a Kadir. That just about sums up my life."

"Oh, no, you don't." She threw her hands on her hips. "I don't know much about the Kadirs, except what little Tarik told me. And even if I did, that wouldn't tell me anything about you. Spill."

Ah, hell. He hated talking about himself. But there didn't seem any way out of it now without making her an enemy instead of a comrade.

Grimacing, he cleared his throat. "The Kadirs are an ancient tribe—originally nomads—bedouins. We don't belong to any particular country, but most countries have welcomed us over the centuries because we're fair tradesmen. A few hundred years ago, Zabbarán was on our family's trade route and we ended up in a drawn-out battle with the local savages, the Taj Zabbar."

"So you still hate them? Wow, now that's holding a grudge."

"We don't hate them. They hate us. Um…" The family feud was based on a long story that she didn't really need to hear. "I guess you know that a few years ago, the Taj Zabbar rebelled against their neighbors, the Kasht, and retook control of their country—then they struck oil and got rich."

"I think I heard about that on the news, yeah. And didn't I also hear something about the international community warning them not to proceed with their plans to go nuclear?"

Swallowing past his dry throat, he nodded. "What most people don't know is that the Taj Zabbar have sworn to destroy the Kadir family, in any way they can. They kicked off their little vendetta against us by causing an explosion in America that killed a handful of members of our family. And, by the way, that explosion also killed and maimed a couple of dozen innocent people. And to top it all off, the Taj made it look like the explosion was our fault."

He lowered his voice, not sure he could get past the rest of this part of his life story. "My father was killed that day, too.

The surprise attack alerted my entire family to the danger. And changed my life forever."

"I was about to tell you to skip over the family and get down to your story." Her eyes filled with sorrow. "But you just did. In a huge way. I'd heard about the explosion a while back. I'm so sorry about your father."

"Me, too. His death taught me a lot more about revenge than I ever wanted to know."

They walked on in silence for a few minutes, allowing him time to push the images of that horrible experience back into his memory banks. Glancing up the trail, he spotted the summit and automatically turned his head to check the secondary peaks surrounding their position.

There. Unexpectedly, just off to their left, he spotted something that gave him a chill down the back of his neck. A glint of sunlight—which had to be bouncing off binoculars or a rifle scope.

Chapter 3

"Run!"

"What the…?" Morgan didn't have time to take a breath. Karim jerked her around, pulling her behind him as he tore up the last incline to the peak.

At the summit and out of breath, she planted her feet and reared her arm back out of his grasp. "Stop. Before I go another step, tell me what's wrong."

Karim dragged in air as his lips spread in a wide grin. "Someone was watching us." He pointed back the way they'd come.

"What?" Spinning three-sixty degrees, she sent quick glances to the various sandstone ridges and spires surrounding them. "I don't see anyone."

"I did. Someone had us in their sights, watching us through binoculars or a scope." When she raised her eyebrows at the idea, he went on, "Look, you're going to have to learn to trust me. I'm the designated bodyguard. I've had specialized awareness and cultural training. From now on, if you're going to succeed with your mission and live to return home, when I say jump, you hop to it."

If he hadn't said the words with the most ridiculously boyish expression on his face, she might have let him have it. The first grin had made him more than a bodyguard. The second one made him gorgeous. He was almost too charming for his own damn good. The commanding words and the endearing grin did not match up.

She decided to go with the endearing side. Karim was starting to get under her skin. That story about his father being killed in an explosion had changed her original opinions, and now she wanted to know more about this man. Not to mention the fact that she actually did need his help to reach the successful completion of their mission.

"All right. So, what's next, then?"

"We've made good time so far." His cautious glance left her face and shot backward down at the valley from where they'd just come. "But I think we'd better start scouting for a place to camp. A hot meal and a few hours' sleep will keep us going longer."

"It'll probably be dark in an hour or so," she remarked. "Do you really think we can push on during the middle of the night?"

"We've had the training and we have the equipment. I think if we're careful, the two of us can do the same things we'd planned on doing with a four-man team."

Morgan shrugged and threw up her hands. "Lead on, then."

It didn't take Karim long to find a proper campsite. A spot hidden among oversized boulders. Located in a rock formation sheltered from the winds—and away from anyone's overly ambitious curiosity—he liked the privacy and the level ground.

But he didn't care for the continuing feeling that someone was watching them. It gave him a bad case of nervous energy he'd rather do without. He needed to be the steady one, the rock, to smooth over any rough spots on the trip so Morgan could do her job.

As she rolled out her sleeping bag and he pulled together the right-size rocks for their small campfire, he went over the possibilities in his head. If their observer or observers were part of a Taj Zabbar military patrol, he and Morgan would already have been fired upon or—worse—surrounded and captured. But, if not them, then who?

He didn't like the idea of unknown persons wandering around nearby, potentially interfering with their mission. It was bad enough learning that Taj patrols were combing this isolated section of their country for unknown reasons. Too many unanswered questions.

Morgan would hate the idea of such dangling details. She might even scrap the mission. So they wouldn't talk about anything to do with the mission for now. He would keep her mind on other things instead.

Checking the wind currents to be sure any accidentally released smoke would not give away their position, Karim dug into his pack for his BlastMatch Fire Starter and camp stove.

"Don't forget to scout the area for any reptiles before setting up." That ought to take her mind off the mission temporarily.

She twisted her head and threw him a skeptical look. "Come now, don't get too cute. I attended the class on desert wildlife, the same as you. There might be a poisonous lizard or asp near a water hole, but not many at this altitude. Nothing much lives here."

Well, that served him right. "I noticed during training that you seemed fairly competent with the camping instructions and not overly nervous about sleeping in the wild. Have you done a lot of outdoor work, then?"

Plopping down on her sleeping bag, Morgan reached for the water and took a drink before answering. It gave him time to admire her again. Her thick, dark lashes surrounding clear, green eyes. The slight shoulders running down to a narrow waist. She might be dressed as a bedouin male, but her feminine form was abundantly clear to anyone who paid attention.

And he'd been paying too much attention. Turning back to his stove, he proceeded with the setup.

"Not a lot of time outdoors, no," she answered. "Most of my kind of work is done in the cities and metropolises of the world. But I grew up on a ranch in Wyoming. Spent all of my childhood on the back of a horse with a rifle in my hand. I was a real tomboy."

"Tomboy?" He wasn't sure he understood the term.

"You didn't grow up in America, did you?" She grinned at him, and he forgot what they'd been talking about.

Pulling himself together, he managed, "No. I grew up on various islands in the Mediterranean. My father was the president of the Kadir family's shipping business. But I attended university at MIT. That's in Massachusetts."

"I know." Her eyes sparkled in the last of the setting sun. "And I could've guessed you went someplace like MIT. Anyway, a tomboy is a little girl who prefers being outside and getting dirty to playing with dolls and wearing fancy dresses."

"And that was you? You liked getting dirty? In a way, I could've guessed that, too."

The smile faded from her face as she sat up on her knees. "I'd better see to my rifle before the sunlight is completely gone."

Sitting back, he let the stove's fire mature as he watched her carefully open her specially made case and remove a stock and barrel. Then she dug into her case again for a soft polishing cloth and oil. In moments she'd dismantled the rest of the rifle's components and began lovingly rubbing and inspecting the tool of her deadly trade.

As her fingers trailed along the gleaming, mahogany stock, Karim's errant mind dived right into sensual territory—though he knew better. He pictured what those fingers could do as they trailed over the various parts of his body that by now had grown hard at the mere idea of her attentions.

Clearing his throat, he glanced away. He had a feeling rest periods might become the most difficult part of the entire trip.

Karim turned out to be a decent cook, though that hadn't been one of his original duties on their mission. He'd made them a tasty makeshift dinner on his tiny camp stove. After a few hours sleep, Morgan awoke feeling good, rested and ready to travel. Most of all, she was more intrigued with the man than ever.

"I don't think we'll need the NVGs to navigate the trail tonight." He doused their fire and then stopped to stare up at the heavens.

Morgan glanced up, too, and was surprised to find enough light to see every detail of their surroundings. "Wow. I don't think I've ever seen the stars so bright. Not even in Wyoming on a clear night."

She set to work packing her bedroll and making sure her rifle was all set for desert travel. "It feels odd starting out before midnight. Odd and a little chilly."

"You'll need your jacket."

Gritting her teeth, she held her tongue. He was taking this bodyguarding business to heart, and she didn't want to spoil either the mission or their budding relationship by being a smart mouth. And though she was tempted to leave her jacket in her pack just to spite him, she dragged out the black Gore-Tex and shrugged into the sleeves like a good girl. Letting her muscles go cold could make them seize up. Not the best plan for maintaining flexibility.

As they started down the path, the three-quarter moon appeared suddenly over a distant peak. "Geez, with all that moon glow, it's nearly daylight at this altitude."

"Yeah," he said on a breath. "I don't like it. Our original plan called for the cover of darkness.

"Uh… Hold up a second." He stopped at a wide point on the trail, ducked out of his backpack and soon found whatever he was searching for in the pockets. "The NVGs won't help spot snipers in the rocks, but this thermal vision scope could make a difference."

Another toy. She held in the chuckle.

He raised the instrument to his eye and slowly scouted the area. "Nothing yet. But let me show you how to use this. Just in case you need it."

She got a ten-minute lesson on how the scope would pick up the heat from a person's body temperature and read their presence even at a distance of several hundred yards.

But before she finished checking their immediate area, Karim said, "I feel someone watching us again. But they're too good to let themselves be spotted. You keep the thermal imager and check it periodically."

"What are you going to be doing?"

The rustling noises of Karim digging in his pack ended with a familiar click. The sound of a gun stock being locked into place was something Morgan would recognize in her sleep. She dropped the hand holding the thermal imager and turned.

"Holy Mother of…" Closing her gaping mouth, she stood,

watching with fascination as he fit a thirty-round magazine into a state-of-the-art KAC 6x35mm PDW.

Morgan didn't know much about high-tech toys, but she knew about guns. All kinds of guns. And the Knight's Armament 6x35mm Personal Defense Weapon was the king of killing machines. Ultralightweight and compact, the experimental design didn't require much finesse. Just point and shoot and nothing within three hundred meters would live to tell the tale.

As he adjusted the weapon's strap over his shoulder, Karim looked up at her with dancing, flirty eyes. "You keep watch. I'll be ready for anything." His deep baritone voice rolled over her in waves of lustful power.

Maybe it was the appreciation for such an excellent piece of hardware that he saw in her eyes. Or maybe it was the fire that had been ignited low in her belly by the mere sight of his handsome, bronzed face, grown even darker with a five o'clock shadow, that made all the difference.

Whatever it was that had pushed him over the edge, Karim sprang to his feet and took her in his arms. Before she could react, he kissed her. An openmouthed kiss. His tongue sought her tongue with sudden, desperate need. Without any hesitation on her part, she threw her arms around his neck and held on for the ride.

Strong hands. Firm mouth. She'd known all along his kiss would be a little rough. A lot like fireworks. She felt herself exploding in a shower of wanting.

She hadn't realized how much desire had built up between them until she responded to his low, sensual groan with a deep-throated moan of her own. Dear Lord, the man could kiss.

And more. There was something else, silent but acute, going on between them. It made her hungry to find out what, and she was never hungry. Never ready in an instant to demand everything from a man.

Deepening the kiss, his warm mouth welcomed her response. Tasting and exploring, he built the fire to nearly unbearable heights.

His hands wandered down her body, rubbing her shoulders, then down her arms. Moving lower, his fingers gently brushed her rib cage at the very edge of her already tender breasts. Finally, his palms cupped her bottom. With fingers splayed possessively, he drew her tight against his erection.

She gasped, jumped and pressed her belly even closer as her fingernails automatically dug into his shoulders, allowing her to hang on instead of spinning off the planet. Her whole body was on fire.

Just like that? How could this be? She had to catch her breath. Clear her head. Find some sanity.

All of a sudden, the horrible images that fouled her dreams on most nights and that she'd worked so hard to banish came back to strike a chilling blow to her ardor.

Stiffening, she broke the kiss and stepped away. Karim didn't fight her.

He looked shell-shocked and breathless as his dark, endless eyes stared into hers. Exactly the way she felt.

Then he sobered. "Um… Hell. That was pretty intense."

"Yeah," was all she could manage. Her heart was pounding in her chest; so hard, she wondered if it would jump right out her throat.

"I didn't mean for that to happen. But…" He struggled for words. "That wasn't a simple kiss."

"Nothing simple about that kiss at all."

"What do you want to do about it?"

She knew how much the mission meant. To everyone involved. "The smart thing would be to forget it."

"Is that what you want to do?"

Without answering him directly, she said, "Go on with the mission. As we travel, we can think it over. Separately."

"Is that what you want?"

"No. Not at all." She almost reached out for him.

What she wanted was another kiss, this time initiated by her. More heat. Another blaze, all-consuming and all-powerful.

Karim took a step back. "Me neither. But it would be for the best. When the mission is over, we can get together, like a post-mission debriefing, and talk over our separate thoughts."

Not a chance.

"Fine." It was all she could do to force her trembling fingers to readjust the straps to her pack and rifle case in preparation to move out.

This time, as they traveled down the wider path, Karim stayed a few steps out in front. He advised her to stick close to the limestone cliff walls while he walked point.

Traversing down the pathways in this slightly separated manner gave her a chance to think. But her thoughts remained jumbled.

She'd seen the shock of his own actions reflected in Karim's eyes. He hadn't expected to kiss her like that any more than she'd been ready for it. Well, that was one thing they had in common.

She doubted if they shared very much else.

No, the biggest problem for her seemed to be that he was a temptation. One that she had a feeling would probably overcome her regular reserve by the end of this mission. But he was also not what she wanted on a long-term basis. She'd had plenty of chances to be with adrenaline-pumping, muscle-loaded men who would jump at a chance at a kiss during her years of working for the CIA. But she hadn't, and for a good reason.

Men like Karim didn't stick. Too soon they were off to the next mission or the next dangerous situation.

That wasn't who she was now. Actually, deep down, that was never who she'd been. Circumstances had conspired to keep her going from one mission to the next, never settling down.

Never giving herself a moment to think about the past.

But now that her parents had both died and left her with her grandparent's ranch, she was ready to make a home. A nest. Without her parents there, she wouldn't necessarily have to think about the past. Only about a new future.

Lost as she was in contemplation, when the first shot rang out and echoed around the canyon walls, she dropped to a crouch in shock. But in less than a second she sat up, blinking and gasping.

Karim had gone down, too. Only he didn't spring back up.

Crawling toward his prone body, she snatched the KAC PDW at his side and blindly began spraying fire in a huge arc. Another shot rang out.

Gotcha, you fool. Now knowing the sniper's position, she didn't need to waste many more bullets before the weapon's fire stopped altogether, and silence once again reigned on the trail.

Too silent. Ohmygod. Was Karim badly injured? Or had the sniper's bullet stopped him for good?

Chapter 4

Still as a rock and with his face ashen—blue in the moonlight—Karim looked dead when Morgan reached his side. Leaning over him, she bent close enough to feel his warm breath against her cheek.

He was alive. Thank God.

With her chest tight and her throat clogged with fear for his life, she took a moment trying to judge where he'd been hit. There wasn't any blood. None that she could see. So where…?

Then she spotted it. A huge, burned-black bullet hole right in the middle of his chest. But no blood.

Ripping frantically at the straps of his pack and the tapes holding his high-tech water-containment system, she finally removed them and, with trembling fingers, set to work unbuttoning his shirt. One button was all it took for her to realize what had happened.

Karim had been wearing a Kevlar vest.

She sighed deep, full of gratitude for his precautions. He started to moan, gasping and jerking as if he wanted to sit up.

"Stay still," she whispered. "You probably need medical attention."

But if he did, she wasn't sure how they could reach it.

He gulped in more air and groaned. "Hell... Hurts like a bitch."

"Stay still," she repeated. "You've been hit."

"No..." he stammered "...vest. Be okay."

Damn, but she sure hoped so. Her heart and head were thundering as if it'd been her that had taken the hit.

"Need... Need..." He blinked and tried to focus on her face.

"Water." Of course. She helped raise his head so he could drink.

He reached out and grabbed her arm. "Help me to my feet."

"Not yet. Lie still. You may have internal injuries."

"The snip..." He coughed and groaned again. "What happened?"

"I took the sniper out. A single gunman."

"Watching... Waiting for his chance." Karim shifted and bit his lip. "We need to move... Cover." But every time he tried to roll, the pain seemed to smack him back down.

"Easy. Take it easy. Just lie there for a few minutes. Maybe the pain will back off. Give me a chance to look around." She started to rise, checking in every direction.

"My...job." His voice had grown so faint she could barely hear him anymore.

She stopped, leaned close again. "I know it's your job. But let me handle things this one time. I won't go far."

Her chest was on fire in sympathy. He probably wasn't fatally injured. Just hurting badly. She felt his pain as if it were her injury. But there wasn't a lot she could do for him. And a man like this would not be an easy patient. He needed to stay quiet for a few hours.

Karim stirred again. Groaned. Cursed in a language she didn't understand. But she knew the sentiment very well.

Were they in danger here? Would that sniper's buddies come looking for him soon? She concentrated for the moment on what that sniper must've been all about. He had obviously been tracking them for hours. Maybe since they'd first entered the mountains. Did he have a way of communicating with his compatriots?

A cell wouldn't work around these cliffs. And the probability seemed slim that a lone man, a man without an army platoon to back him up in this isolated country, would have access to a satellite phone.

No doubt he'd been a sentry. One who might not be missed for days. She hoped.

Morgan came to the conclusion that they should have at least a few hours before anyone would check. She hoped that was all the time Karim would need to get on his feet. It would have to do.

Glancing down the trail, she noticed a switchback ahead. The path made a natural turn around a cluster of boulders. A tiny flat spot out of the winds might not be as comfortable as their earlier rest stop had been, but it would keep them sheltered until morning.

Now, how to get him there? She didn't want to waste a lot of time. The only solution that came to her in a hurry was to lay out her sleeping bag, put Karim on it and drag him down to the switchback.

Walking the path, she kicked any small rocks or pebbles aside. Then she came back for Karim. His eyes were closed, but the grimace of pain was still apparent on his face.

She took his arm lightly. "I found a spot where we can rest for bit. But I'll need your help reaching it."

He tried to sit up again, but the pain drove him down with a grunt. She laid out the bag. And took a deep breath.

"This may hurt some, but can you turn on your side? I'll help. You roll nice and easy and I'll do the rest."

She could see the effort it took to do as she requested written on his face. Another sympathy pain nearly doubled her over, but she knew what they had to do. She helped him roll, and, between them, they had him on his side fairly quickly. Then came the hard part. Taking off his pack. The damn thing weighed almost as much as she did.

Lots of huffing and puffing later, Karim was finally free of the pack, his water containment system and the heavily damaged vest, and now he was lying quietly on her sleeping bag. She picked up the tufted edges of the bag and tugged. Nothing. It took her longer to get the bag moving down the path than any of the rest of it had taken. But after making the first advancement, she let gravity assist in the rest.

At last, after a lot of hard breathing and massive sweating in the dropping temperatures, she had him cocooned inside the natural-rock wind barrier. She dropped down on her knees to whisper to him.

"We're safe for a while. Can you rest?"

"Amazing… You did it." He started to shake. "Cold."

She put her hand on his forehead. He was feverish, but didn't seem to be burning up. She used his bedroll as a blanket.

"How are you going to stay warm?" he asked weakly.

She watched him fight to ease into a more comfortable position and still be able to see her face.

"I'll be fine." She planned to stay awake, watching over him. In the event he had internal injuries, she would find a way to abort the mission. Get him to civilization by some means.

"As long as we're not moving, need to share our body heat. Below freezing before sunup. Com… Come over here."

A knot of panic, twisted by worry over him, rolled in her stomach and threatened to take her over an edge. But he was right about needing body heat. They'd learned that lesson in desert survival school. She would have to push her old terror aside.

Moving carefully, Morgan slid in behind him as he lay on his side. Karim's big body shivered as she pressed close.

"Closer," he murmured. "We need the warmth."

She almost smacked his arm before remembering his condition. "Are you sure you're hurt?"

He chuckled and groaned at the same time. "My choice would be the other way around. Me spooning you. But my ribs still hurt like the devil."

She flattened against him and hugged as close as she dared. "Okay?"

"Better. Warmer. But talk to me. Keep me awake."

"You need sleep to heal."

"Not yet. If I start coughing, I want to make sure there's no blood."

Oh, man. If he did start coughing, she figured the pain from the bruising would be excruciating. But coughing up blood would be so much worse. That could mean internal injuries. A collapsed lung. Or who knew what disaster.

"Okay. What do you want to talk about?"

"Not the…kiss. Not yet."

"Yeah. I'm with you there. So how about telling me why you came on this mission?"

Karim had never in his wildest imagination thought he'd be attracted to a hard-as-nails woman. But damned if Morgan Bell, with her willowy frame and nerves of steel, wasn't the sexiest woman he'd ever met. When he'd been a boy, before his father died and his mother had committed suicide, he remembered her as possessing the same bottomless patience and underlying strength as he now recognized in Morgan.

But he didn't think of his mother when he saw Morgan. Not in the least.

"I came on the mission because my family needed me." Only partially the truth. He hoped she wouldn't ask more.

"Not good enough."

There. See? The woman could read his mind.

"Back in survival training I got the feeling you hadn't been on many missions," she added. "Why this one?"

He felt her breath, warm and sensual, on his neck. Her breasts were flattened against his back. The aching bruise on his chest all but disappeared from his thoughts, but he refused to dwell on the erotic impulses that had taken over in its place.

"This might not be the best time to tell you," he began with some trepidation. "But I've been training for over a year for a mission. This one was just the first that came up. Field operations are not my regular work."

"I sort of knew that without having to be told." She snuggled closer and wrapped her loose arm around his. "I would be willing to wager your regular work has something to do with technical stuff."

"Yes, well, you're right. But I was absolutely ready for this assignment. I won't let you down."

"I don't doubt it for a moment."

She sounded convinced, but he couldn't see her expression— her eyes. He wanted to explain why it mattered. He wouldn't be divulging anything too personal, but she needed to understand his devotion to the job.

"Do you know anything about the situation that started this journey? About the child that was taken?"

"My mission is to kill the target. I'm not sure I need…"

"Did it bother you, being forced to kill that Taj sniper on the trail?" He wasn't sure why the question had popped out suddenly. "Are you okay with having to take the shot?"

"I'm all right," she whispered after a few moments. "Killing from a distance is my job. I've found it doesn't help anything if I think too much."

"Do you like your work?" He wouldn't question the morality of the occupation, choosing to believe she didn't kill for fun or profit.

"I'm good at it. But no, I don't really like my work. In fact, this will be my last mission. I'm quitting. I'm only here as a favor to your cousin Tarik."

He would've liked to ask what she planned to do next in life. What did hired killers do after they stopped? But he wanted to see her face for such a conversation. And as much as he was turned on by having her snugged up against his back, this was not the time for wistful, face-to-face talks of a future.

Gritting his teeth in an effort to erase the idea of flipping over and kissing her senseless, he thought instead about the mission. "I'm here because of that little boy—Matin. Neither he nor his parents did anything to deserve what happened. They just became pawns in some nasty, political game the Taj Zabbar are playing."

"His parents were killed?"

"It started a while back when my cousins captured one of the Taj elders. Tarik and the CIA have been trying to make the elder tell what he knows about the tribe's nuclear plans. In the meantime, the Taj have been threatening to make trouble if the elder is not immediately released, but we thought it was of no concern. We thought we'd taken precautions. That we were safe.

"Then the Taj sent agents to storm an apartment in Turkey where several Kadir families were living." Karim had to stop, swallow, to go on. "Matin's mother and father resisted, killing one of the Taj agents. But they died before they could save their son. Little Matin has been in the hands of the elder Nabil Talal for nearly a month now."

That was another mental image Karim could've done without. Nabil Talal was widely recognized as a madman.

"I take it they are asking for a trade." Morgan's voice was gruff, determined. "Do we know for certain the boy is still alive?"

"We've had clandestine agents inside Zabbarán for years. They tell us the boy's alive and located in one of Talal's fortresses, staying with the elder's mother."

"How are you feeling now? Is the pain any better?"

"Much better. Do you want to start moving again? I think I can make it." He wouldn't know for sure how bad his ribs hurt until he tried to stand.

"Not yet. Let's stay warm for another hour or two. Keep talking. I want to make new plans on our revised schedule."

Karim wasn't sure he had ever heard anyone so…set on killing. But it didn't keep him from wanting to kiss her. To take her in his arms and soothe out the frown lines he guessed were forming on her forehead.

He had wanted adventure. Wanted to find a better way to even the score with the Taj. Wanted to be a risk taker for a change. But Morgan Bell might be one risk he hadn't taken into account.

Chapter 5

Morgan blinked the sleep out of her eyes, chagrined that she'd actually fallen asleep when she'd wanted to keep watch over Karim. Worse yet, deep gray light was already filtering in through crevices and fissures in the craggy rocks. It was nearly dawn.

She rolled, reaching for Karim. Only to find that his side of the bedroll was empty. Sitting straight up and checking around, she found him standing nearby. Through her half-lidded, still-drowsy eyes, she watched him grimacing as he hunched his shoulders enough to slip into what was left of the water-containment system. Last night's shot had taken out the center bladder of the system, but plenty of water remained in the other two compartments.

Her shoulders ached with wanting to assist him in his efforts. The physical pain, suddenly so strong and clear in her own body, pulled her up short. Air hitched in her throat as a full realization of what had been happening to her finally hit. This was empathy. True empathy for another's pain, deep enough and strong enough to make her body miserable.

Real, raw emotion. She hadn't felt anything like it in so many years, she'd almost given up hope of ever finding it again.

Why now? Why him?

True, there was a lot to like about Karim. His dark, swarthy looks. That single dimple in his chin. The richness of his voice. His flash of humor, along with the sharp, sensual lust that often lit his penetrating, midnight eyes.

More than all that. Something about his need to protect. To save. It tore at her normal reserve and desire for isolation. Here was a man with no wish to harm. None. Yes, she believed he would stand up for what was right. Take a life but only when pushed to the brink. And then only to save an innocent.

In her eyes, he was more than a little appealing. But, through it all, she still saw his blinding need for adrenaline and the demand building behind those sexy eyes to fling caution to the wind and jump into the flames. Like he'd jumped out of the helicopter and into a sandstorm. It was an interesting phenomenon when directed at her. Otherwise, the whole idea scared her to death.

Her life needed to be controlled. Planned out. He represented the exact opposite.

"You're finally up," he grunted as he gingerly tapped down Velcro tabs across his chest.

"So are you." She scrambled off the sleeping bag. "Why didn't you wake me so I could help you with that?"

"You can help with my pack in a minute. Want something to eat before we get started?"

Shaking her head, she replied, "Water and a protein bar and I'm good."

He moved carefully, slowly, as he dug into his backpack. The man was in pain but wouldn't give up.

"Don't," she pleaded. "I can get it."

Holding up his hand, palm facing out to make her stop, he said, "I'm not an invalid. Let me do my job."

Stubborn. This guy was chock-full of interesting characteristics.

"I've been thinking about how the plans have changed," he said through gritted teeth. "I believe there's a way to cut a couple hours off our time. Get us closer to being on track."

Taking the bar he offered, she tore open the wrapper. "I'm afraid to ask."

He gave her a raised-eyebrow look. "I'm in perfect shape. A little pain can't slow me down. And we're better off staying close to the timetable the team originally devised."

Swallowing past the lump of protein bar, she said, "Okay. So what do you want to do?"

"A village, maybe a couple thousand people, is about an hour's walk from here. It's a bit off our planned track. But if we can get there early enough, I'm betting we can find an unattended Jeep to commandeer. That'll accomplish a couple of things.

"First..." He held up one finger. "It should throw off whoever comes looking for that gunman you shot. We won't be traveling the regular goat trail down the mountain pass and will be a lot harder for anyone to spot.

"And second..." He grinned as he held up two fingers. "It should give us a considerable jump on getting to the meeting place."

"Steal a Jeep? You can do that?"

He shrugged. "If it's mechanical, I can figure it out."

Morgan struggled with her better judgment. Did she try to rein him back in and go with a more practical plan? Or did she follow him off the virtual cliff and risk the entire mission on a *maybe?*

After swallowing the bar and washing it down with water,

she came to a conclusion. She had wanted to change her life, hadn't she? Well, deviating from the straight and narrow was the first big change she could make.

"All right, I'm in." She waded up the wrapper and carefully stashed it in her pack. "How fast a pace can you set?"

"Help me with my backpack." He hefted the pack with considerable care and handed it over for her help. "The trail is all downhill from here. How quickly can you move?"

Smiling inside, she decided against being outwardly smug while she eased the pack on his back. "Set the pace. I'll manage to keep up somehow."

Forty-five minutes later, Karim was wondering if he'd lost his mind. Last night's pain was only a faint memory. His lung capacity still seemed good. But his normal high-endurance level appeared to be failing him as the two of them scrambled over granite massifs and skirted deep abysses.

He was having some trouble keeping up with Morgan. Luckily, he'd thought to stuff his climbing gloves into his pack at the last moment. Otherwise, he'd have bloodied hands from grabbing knobby rock abutments and finding finger jams for support.

At this point he'd already slipped once, catching himself with one hand against the sharp detritus on the descent path. The rope burns he'd suffered by helping Morgan rappel past a basalt outcropping too steep to descend by foot stung like fire. And he'd been forced to crab-walk down a deep, rock chimney, scraping his backpack along with his calves.

Was this his great new plan? Must be sunstroke.

"Wait." Morgan put her hand on his arm. "Listen."

They were within a quarter mile of the mountain village, and the everyday noises made by a population who spent most of their time outdoors should be echoing up and down the cliffs and canyons. He supposed she could've easily been hearing the sounds of their morning market. And of men readying for work at their stone cutting or other trades. But those normal, sunup sounds would mean it was already too late in the day for him to do any skulking around looking for unattended vehicles. So be it. He would have to think of something else.

As the first hysterical shouts reached his ears, though, he knew the muffled sounds they'd been hearing were anything but normal. Then he heard shots fired. More shots. Then explosions. More yelling.

"What is it?" Morgan whispered with an edge of panic in her voice. "What's happening?"

"Wait here. I'll try to get closer and find out."

She grabbed on to his sleeve, wouldn't let go. "Not a chance. You're not leaving me."

Torn between his duty to keep her safe and his desire to complete their mission, Karim hesitated. But they had little choice. They'd come this far down the mountain. Climbing back would be impossible for Morgan with her limited knowledge of rock-climbing technique. The only way lay ahead.

The village was situated on a wide bluff, backed up against the butte, with roads going off in three directions. They'd been approaching from a northwesterly position. However, a small deviation would keep them in the cliffs above the village and away from the roads.

"All right. Let's see if we can't find an overlook where we can get a view down at the village without being seen."

Morgan used her special GPS unit and pointed out the direction. He just hoped to hell that way was passable.

Within fifteen minutes, they'd found an ancient, navigable lava flow that led them right to the edge of a tall cliff. By now, the hard, brash desert sun beat down on every surface, giving little relief to whatever plant or reptile might be trying to survive in such harsh conditions.

As he wiped away a trickle of sweat, Karim looked out and noticed smoke coming from the village. Grabbing his image-stabilized, long-range binoculars from the pack, he studied the scene in the distance below them.

"Taj soldiers," he said on a low breath. "They're burning houses. Tearing down the market stalls. Firing on the people."

"Their *own* people? Why?"

"With the Taj there's no telling."

She hunched her shoulders and blinked. "Let me see."

The scene in the glasses became so bloody and vile that he hesitated. "I'm not sure that's a good idea." He lowered the binoculars and shook his head softly.

Morgan glanced back and forth, checking his expression and staring down at the burning village in the distance. "No one has ever thought to shelter me from facing something horrible. This is a first. I don't know how I feel about that."

He could see the conflicting emotions play out on her face. Staying silent, he let her make the final decision.

"I don't need to check the scene now," she finally agreed. "But we need to climb down there quickly so we can help the people. I'm guessing the troops aren't sparing women and children."

Shaking his head again, more firmly now, he said, "All I see are men, but that doesn't mean anything. And going down there now is not a good idea. This is an internal Taj problem. We can't be involved. We're not even supposed to be in their country. The soldiers will kill us on sight. And if they don't, the Taj villagers might kill us themselves."

But it was possible that whatever motive had brought this trouble within the Taj tribe could be used to their ultimate advantage.

"Wait." He glanced again through the binoculars. "The

soldiers are leaving. Looks like they're taking all the motorized vehicles they can find. So much for stealing a Jeep."

"Do you see any animals? Horses?"

Scanning the scene, he spotted a blind canyon in the distance. It would've been out of the view of the soldiers.

"The villagers seem to be grazing some sort of animals in that canyon to your right. But I can't quite tell what kind. My first guess would be goats. Maybe they also keep a horse or two."

He gave the village a once-over through the glasses again. Saw nothing moving but noted fires continued to smolder unattended. A few vehicles lay charred and abandoned on their sides on the roads.

"Let's go find out." Confusion left Morgan's face and her expression returned to her usual, determined scowl.

After giving her idea some thought, he decided checking out the possibility would be worth the slight detour. *If* they could get in and out without being seen.

"All right," he murmured. "But you stay behind me. And do exactly as I tell you. No questions. Agreed?"

She nodded, apparently deciding only one of them could be in charge at a time.

"Fine. Check the maps for the best route."

They found a drop-off into a canyon to their right with easily navigated, natural steps down to the floor of the bluff. He was grateful they didn't have to skirt past the village so Morgan wouldn't have to face the carnage. But it took them nearly a half hour to sneak into the blind canyon where the animals were being kept in open pens.

As they crept along, the overpowering stench of burning wood, gasoline and other underlying smells he would rather not think about, reached his nostrils. He remained quiet, hoping Morgan would not insist on going closer to inspect the scene.

But she never deviated from their immediate goal, the animals in the canyon. "You were right. They're grazing long-eared goats." She'd made the statement with disappointment in her voice.

"Yes, but look over there near the water tank." He pointed toward the shadows at the far wall of the canyon.

"Camels."

Checking over his shoulder and then to the right and left, Karim started out toward a small herd of about six camels. Staked in the shade of a cliff, they were quiet next to a stock tank and a small, concrete block building.

"Hold on." Morgan came up beside him. "Do you know how to ride a camel?"

"Not a clue. But I've seen it done on the internet."

"Yeah, that'll be a big help. I'm hoping it's a little like riding a horse."

He didn't want her to know, but he had little knowledge of how to ride a horse, either. Camel, horse. What difference did it make?

Despite all his cautioning before they began, about letting him lead, he stepped back and let her go her own way. She went straight to the tank, plunged her hand in and brought back a palm full of water. Moving quickly, she offered the water to the nearest camel.

The animal grunted but lapped up the water with big, rubbery lips.

"There you go. You and I are going to be buddies, aren't we?" She rubbed the camel's neck.

Turning back to Karim, she whispered, "These animals have been staked using bits and harnesses. All we'll need are blankets and saddles."

Plus a lesson on how to saddle a camel would be much appreciated. "I read somewhere camels are fussy. They spit."

Morgan didn't seem to be paying attention to him. "Make friends with one," she said over her shoulder as she moved toward the concrete building.

Friends? "What do they eat? Should I feed them?"

She stopped with her hand on the door. "I believe they're a kind of a cross between horse and cow. They give milk, graze and chew cud. Why don't you try cutting up an apple and offering it to that one?"

By the time she returned, lugging a couple of small saddles, he had come to the conclusion that apples weren't their idea of snack food. But he had managed to get one to take a handful of salt bush.

Between the two of them, he and Morgan figured out how to saddle and mount the camels. She looked spectacular sitting in the saddle. Chin high. Back straight. He knew without the bedouin head scarf, her long, lush hair would've been streaming down her back in a proud mane. She'd said she had been a tomboy in her youth. But obviously she still knew how to sit astride an animal.

He just wished he were as competent.

But he managed. Though he was glad no one else was around to watch his comedic attempts at making the camel do his bidding.

"What direction?" Morgan asked as they left the canyon and entered the open desert range.

"Not back toward the village." He didn't want to take any chances of being spotted by someone who could make trouble. He also didn't want to chance rattling Morgan by any of the sights.

He wanted her safe. Unperturbed by events. Ready to do her job. In another day they would arrive at the meeting spot. Then it wouldn't take long to set up her shot.

Nodding to the right, he gave her his best opinion. "The

road that keeps going right heads down a short pass and ends on the desert floor. That's our best bet."

She nodded and turned her mount in that direction. Within minutes they entered the pass. It was all Karim could do to control his animal and keep up.

They moved quietly, save for the sound of animals' hooves against the rock, for a few minutes until Karim's skin suddenly began to crawl. The thundering quiet made him jerk his head up as he sought out the lines of the cliffs overhead.

But it was too late. He spotted the armed men positioned directly above them and concealed in the rocks too late to make any move to draw his weapon.

"Morgan," he said quietly.

"Yes."

"Don't make any sudden moves. Do not go for your rifle."

"Wha…?" She lifted her eyes and saw the same thing he'd seen. "Why haven't they taken any shots at us?" Her voice was hoarse, raspy.

Like spearfishing in a bathtub. "I don't know."

But they were about to find out. A half dozen horsemen came riding up, surrounding them. They weren't Taj soldiers, but the men all carried rifles. And they looked angry. Uncivilized.

He didn't care what they had in mind for him. But he suddenly discovered that it mattered very much what they did to the woman riding beside him.

Morgan. She was more than his assignment now. He must find a way to keep her safe.

Chapter 6

"This is all my fault." Morgan was muttering under her breath, wishing she'd been smart enough to stick with who she was instead of trying to change.

The men who'd captured them had taken their weapons, then forced them, still on the camels, to a nearby water well in the desert. There she and Karim had been dragged off their beasts, their hands and feet tied, and finally they'd been left side-by-side under a date palm.

"Quiet." Karim's hands were bound to his feet in hog-tied fashion. Her hands and feet had at least been tied separately.

With his head bowed, he looked terribly uncomfortable as he spoke into his knees. "So far, I don't think they know you're a woman. Just keep your mouth shut and maybe they won't find out.

"Besides," he whispered with a hiss. "Nothing is your fault. I'm the guard. It was my screwup."

She couldn't argue the point. Most of their botched mission this far had been his idea. But she shouldn't have allowed him to go on making new plans and blindly following along. In fact, she never should have started out on such a fool's mission with him after the copter landing aborted. She knew better.

"What do they want with us? Who are these men?" She kept her voice low, sure that Karim alone could hear.

"I believe they're bedouins. Probably some of my distant cousins. But I can't make out the dialect.

"And they seem to be waiting for something—or someone," he added quietly.

"I thought Tarik told us that all bedouins had cleared out of Zabbarán over the last six months. Didn't he say they left because the Taj issued death warrants for any nonnational caught in their territory?"

"That was the intel we received." Karim seemed as confused as she was.

Great.

"If these guys are bedouins, they can't be happy with the Taj Zabbar for making them leave their traditional territory. Do you suppose they think we're Taj?"

"If they did…" Karim grunted as he squirmed, trying to get a look at her face. "They would've killed us first and asked questions later."

Morgan swallowed that news hard. He was right again. Yet these men seemed to be building up to something. That couldn't be good.

"What are they doing?" he asked in a soft tone. "Can you see them?"

She glanced up and squinted through the growing dusk past a scraggly bush. A couple of small boulders blocked most of the view to what she supposed was their camp. But she found a spot where she could make out one or two men walking in and out of her field of vision.

"Looks like they may be making dinner," she told him. "I think I smell campfire smoke."

"Good thing bedouins aren't cannibals."

He'd said it so seriously. So quietly. Without a trace of humor in his voice. It took her a moment to get the joke.

Even then, she couldn't manage a laugh. But he'd tried to make her smile, and that thought warmed her heart and helped her relax a little.

He was a good man. Too bad he was also the type of man who would take off over the side of a cliff just for the adrenaline rush and never think twice.

"Do any of them seem to be checking on us while they concentrate on food?" His voice held a note of promise.

"There isn't a guard posted nearby, no. But I would bet they'll have guards at the perimeters of camp. What are you thinking?"

"I'm thinking that they believe we're no threat, tied and guarded. And I'm hoping they keep paying no attention to us.

"We need to be ready," he added softly. "And set to move if we see the chance. Can you do something for me now? Scoot a little closer."

Another wild scheme? Not for her. "Whatever you have in mind, count me out. I'm done following your lead. That's how we ended up where we are now."

He hesitated, but only for a quick second. "Morgan... darling. Listen. If we do nothing, we're probably dead. And if they find out you're a woman, it'll go much worse for you. Then you may wish they had killed you instead of keeping you alive. Trust me. Doing something is better than the alternative in this case."

He'd called her darling. No one—not ever—called her darling.

She didn't trust him. Not anymore. But a slim chance of

survival was better than sure death. What did she have to lose? "Tell me what you have in mind."

"See if you can reach up under the pants leg on my right calf. I've strapped a KA-BAR to my leg with Velcro. If we can get hold of that knife, we can make plans."

Morgan thought she knew what a KA-BAR knife looked like. As she recalled, her father had owned one for hunting. With large, long blades and stacked leather handles, that brand of knife was supposedly popular with United States fighting troops like the marines. And Karim had strapped something like that to his leg? The man definitely qualified as reckless.

Awkward as it was in this position, trying to get both her bound hands up under his pants leg, it took a few minutes to retrieve the knife. She held her breath the whole time.

At last, the swishing noise that Velcro makes when opening told her the knife had come free. "There. Got it. Now what?"

"See if you can saw through the rope between my hands and ankles. But be careful not to cut yourself." His voice was raspy, hoarse.

"What happens if I cut you by accident?" She noted her own voice sounded breathless, winded.

"Easy, sweetheart. No need to rush. Take your time and don't worry about me. I'd say a cut or two would be well worth it at this point."

Perhaps he was right. Nothing to lose.

In the end, it was Morgan who bled. But her injuries came from rope burns to her wrists as she used constant pressure, struggling to cut his bindings loose. She toughed out the small pains. After all, her trigger hand was still in good shape.

At the last cut, Karim sagged a little and then sat up. "Check on the men."

"I can't see anyone, but now I smell food cooking."

He took the knife from her and cut through the ropes binding his ankles with considerably less difficulty and time than her efforts had consumed. Next, they cut each other's hands free. Karim kicked out the kinks and stood.

Rubbing at her sore and bleeding wrists, she waited until the feeling came back into her hands before letting him help her stand, too. They still wore their packs and by now hers felt like several tons of dead weight. She couldn't imagine how Karim was holding up under his much heavier load.

"And now?" she whispered.

"Now we're going to scout around a little. See if there's a lone guard I can overpower so we can skulk away into the dark desert."

That wasn't much in the way of a plan in her opinion. Just sneaking out into the desert wouldn't necessarily mean freedom. The two of them couldn't get very far without weapons or transportation.

Just then she heard a small commotion somewhere nearby, and she recognized the sounds of suddenly restless horses. Maybe the animals had the same feeding and watering times as when the bedouins ate their meals.

"We need to locate the horses," she said forcefully. "Find out where they keep the animals so we can decide if we could cut two out for a getaway without being discovered."

"That's a plan?"

"It's better than no plan at all."

Karim took her by the shoulders and stared into her eyes. "I...might not know how to ride a horse."

Maybe it was the hesitant look she saw in his eyes for the first time. Perhaps it was the rough desire she spotted there as he gazed into hers. Or it might've been the way he gripped her shoulders, telling her he thought she was special. It could've been any of those that did her in.

Whatever it was, she surprised both of them by going up on tiptoes and dragging his mouth down to her level for a kiss.

She nipped her teeth over his bottom lip, then used her tongue to soothe the pain. Fire and ice, she thought. All just part of who she was.

Karim responded with a kiss in return, so deep and full of promise that she nearly lost her balance. Lost her grip on reality. The world spun backward. The sun and the stars shone in the sky at the same time.

But in too few seconds, he tightened his fingers on her shoulders and gently set her back.

Breathing hard, he said, "Later."

No, not later. What had she been thinking—or clearly not thinking? It couldn't happen again—not ever.

"You two finished?" A deep male voice came from behind Karim's back. "If so, may I have a word?"

Karim felt like someone had punched him hard in the jaw, but no one had laid a hand on him yet. Spinning around to face his assailant, he shoved Morgan behind him with one hand and hefted the knife with his other. How could he have left himself vulnerable and unaware? Even in the face of the most astounding kiss imaginable, what kind of guard did that make him?

"You're a Kadir, aren't you?" The man standing before him speaking near-perfect English was about his size. Dark. Swarthy. Dressed in bedouin attire and standing at ease, hands behind his back.

Karim's gut instinct told him truth would be his best choice. "I am Karim Kadir. But who…?"

The fellow stuck out his hand. "I knew it. Pleased to meet a man related to my cousins. I'm known as Kalil, sheik of the bedouin tribe called Malik Zafirah—the victorious.

"My grandfather," he continued as he pinned Karim with

a steely gaze, "was also the maternal ancestor of Tarik, Shakir and Darin Kadir. We welcome the Kadir tribe in our camps."

Karim bent to sheath the knife before clasping the man's hand. "Thanks. But I don't think your men got the word about our welcome. We've been bound for hours."

The sheik smiled warmly. "Sorry, old man. The men knew you were not a known threat, not Taj or another hostile tribe, but strangers to the land. They sent word for me to come and judge whether you were friend or foe."

Karim chewed on that bit of knowledge for a moment. "How did they know? How were you sure I was a Kadir without seeing me?" He waved his hand, indicating his bedouin disguise.

"No offense, Karim Kadir, but there was no mistaking you for anyone but a foreigner. If nothing else," Kalil dropped his gaze to Karim's feet. "The desert boots of a western army soldier gave you away."

Then Sheik Kalil also threw a skeptical glance toward Morgan. "And I am sorry, Miss…Miss…"

"Bell," Karim provided. "Morgan Bell."

"Ms. Bell. It is easy to see that your attire does a disservice to your form. A womanly disguise may have been somewhat more successful in making you appear to be bedouin, but I doubt it."

Karim let the polite snubs slide by. Now that he knew they weren't in harm's way with these men, he had important questions that needed answering.

But before he could ask, Kalil said, "Come join us for a meal. I have a few questions and I suspect I can answer a few of yours. But we must be quick. We cannot linger here for much longer."

Within a couple of hours, Karim was riding through the midnight desert sands on the back of a horse, following unsteadily behind Morgan again. The horse proved only somewhat easier for him to control than the camel. But he couldn't complain. The horses and supplies had been gifts from Sheik Kalil.

Over supper they'd learned from their host that the beginnings of a civil war had been brewing among the normally quiet Zabbarán people over the last few weeks. The sheik claimed that few of the Taj Zabbar population were of the same mind as some of their elders about their country's relations with the rest of the world—or their mission to go nuclear.

Civil unrest and rebel forces were springing up and causing trouble in isolated pockets throughout the country. The bedouin tribes, who had been frequenting these lands for centuries, had joined forces with the rebels against the Taj.

Sheik Kalil's men had ambushed Taj soldiers, the ones who'd pillaged and burned the mountain village yesterday, and beheaded them for their savagery against civilians. When word of that defeat finally reached the heads of the Taj armies, the entire country would erupt in chaos.

On hearing the news, Karim had been ready to abort the mission. One little boy's life would still weigh heavily on his shoulders, but the situation in Zabbarán was far too dangerous for Morgan to continue.

It was Morgan who'd offered a cooler head and a better idea when he'd all but dragged her away from the camp and back into the mountains.

"Is it possible our team may be in the country already and on their way to our original meeting place?" she'd asked. But she didn't wait for his answer. "Let's keep going. We're not that far behind schedule. We can try calling the team once we're there. If they couldn't find a way into Zabbarán because of the civil war, then maybe by now they will have a good extraction plan for getting us out."

Karim had given up in the end. She'd been right, of course. And once Sheik Kalil had learned of their mission, he volunteered to assist them in any way possible.

Thus the horseback ride across the desert in the black of night. Karim had imagined he would break his neck at the pace Morgan set. But after two very fast hours, they arrived at the Zereh Oasis.

Located on the original Spice Road, away from any traffic or human civilization, the Zereh Oasis water well had been contaminated several years back. The vegetation around the well dried up and no one ever stopped there anymore. Still, it was a deserted, rocky space, perhaps a half-mile wide and nearly a mile long, that could offer shelter to a traveler and a place to meet for the Kadir team.

As he and Morgan dismounted and walked the horses to the first cluster of boulders they spotted, Karim noticed spider-like shadows of date palms and dwarf shrub. Their silhouettes appeared in the moonlight like scarecrows of their former forms, dried and spindly in the eerie light. In the stillness of the night, he also thought he could hear a noise, either animal or odd winds, off in distance.

"Do you think the team has arrived before us?" Morgan whispered as she removed her head scarf and shook out her hair.

He shrugged. "We'll have to see. We're a few hours early."

She seemed more concerned with the condition of their mounts than with guessing games. They secured the horses in a natural pen of giant boulders set off to the far side of the main oasis, and then spread Sheik Kalil's gift of hay for the animals to eat.

When they were done, Karim suggested they reconnoiter and scout the oasis. He was determined to find out about those distant noises he'd heard.

Leaving their packs safely under a low, flat granite shelf, they started out across the rocks and dried-out grasses wearing NVGs and communications wires. After several minutes of walking, they happened upon a remarkable discovery. Water, trickling down the side of a sandstone boulder and landing in a natural pool at its base.

"Do you suppose that's good water?" Morgan asked as she moved closer to it.

"I don't think I want to be the first to find out."

He imagined that the water must have begun flowing from these rocks quite some time ago. A large pool had formed and, in the shallow corners, reeds and weeds had already grown several feet tall.

But at that moment, Karim heard another noise that took his attention from the water and sent a chill down his back.

Bending closer to Morgan's ear, he whispered, "Someone else is here. Right beyond those boulders to the left. Don't say a word."

Her eyes grew wide as her lips tightened into a single line.

He motioned for her to wait there as he crept a little closer to the noise. His pulse was racing, his mouth dry as he flattened his body to a boulder and inched into a deep crevice between two rocks. He hoped to hell the noise he'd heard would be their team, waiting for their rendezvous.

What he saw on the far side of the boulder had him swallowing hard and turning to stone. Two Taj soldiers were breaking camp. He'd taught himself the Taj language years ago, but they were speaking so softly that he almost missed the translation.

It seemed the two men were as surprised at finding the water as he'd been. They'd stopped to eat and now needed to move on to rejoin their unit. But one of them sounded determined to fill his water containers before heading out.

Karim slid back into the shadows, made his way quietly over the rocks to Morgan. "Can you swim?"

Before she could reply, he put his hand over her mouth, grabbed her up and waded out into the reeds. Two seconds later they were waist-deep in water with high reeds over their heads. But he could still hear footsteps on the rocks, coming closer.

Chapter 7

The first thing that hit Morgan as Karim shoved her into the water and yanked her under was how frigging cold it felt. For a desert pool warmed by extreme heat during the day, the water in the murky pond could've had ice floating on top. Must be coming from a deep underground spring.

Squatting in the frigid darkness with the water level at the top of her head, she held her breath to the end of her lung capacity. Then she eased her nose and eyes out, looking around through the tangle of weeds. She had to swipe droplets off her NVGs to see anything and then still couldn't see much.

But she could tell Karim was right beside her, his eyes and nose sticking out of the water, too. He moved one finger to his lips, telling her to remain silent.

Easy for him. Her body was already starting to shiver. But she got the idea. Someone had obviously come to the pool to collect water. Someone Karim considered dangerous.

Within moments, her teeth began to chatter. Gritting them

tightly, she wrapped her arms around her waist to conserve warmth. But that didn't help much. Her whole body had started to quake.

Karim reached an arm around her shoulders and tugged her against his chest. "You okay?" he whispered into her ear.

"F-freezing."

Closing both his arms around her back, he cocooned himself around her body, giving them both added warmth. But even with his heroic efforts, she was soon shaking uncontrollably.

"Hang on. It should be okay to get out in a second. The guy's moving away from the pool."

Morgan barely heard Karim over her chattering teeth and the roar of her own blood pounding in her ears. She wasn't sure how he knew when whoever it was had gone. But in a blessed few minutes he pulled her out of the pond and began running his hands over her arms and up and down her back to get the circulation moving again.

In the distance, she heard an engine starting and a vehicle roaring away. Whatever danger had pushed them into the pool must have left the oasis.

Her attention returned to Karim. His gentle caresses and tender ministrations would've been a turn-on—if she could've felt anything. Every muscle, every body part, including her brain, was going numb.

"Your shivering is worse now that we're out of the water in the night air," he muttered. "We need to shed these wet clothes."

It took all her energy to say even one word. "H-here?"

Before she could blink, he swooped her up in his arms and swung around to march off in the direction they'd come. "No. Back to where we left the packs. Nearer to where the horses are staked. Away from the water in case anyone else shows up."

She let him carry her. Let him take the lead in caring for her needs. But she had little choice. Her brain refused to work properly. Every sense, every molecule of her being, focused in on getting warm.

When they reached the clearing where Karim thought they might be safe from anymore unwelcome visitors, he set Morgan on her feet and began stripping off her soaking clothes as quickly as he could. First came the NVGs, the jacket and then the shirt that clung tenaciously to her body, refusing to come unglued from her skin. Next came her boots.

Morgan wasn't too steady on her bare feet. But she huddled into herself and managed to stay upright while he shimmied her wet, sticky pants down her legs. She hung on to him and lifted her feet to kick the pants aside.

As she stood shivering in her bra and panties, it was all he could do to stop staring. The sniper wore pink panties. Think of that.

Then he noticed her skin turning blue and popped himself out of the sensual haze. "Lean against that boulder a sec."

Moving as quickly as possible, he went for his pack and retrieved his bedroll and an extra T-shirt. It took too long to clear a spot of rocks and lay out the bedroll, but he did the best he could as fast as he could.

He used his extra shirt to wipe her down and dry off her hair as much as possible. The shirt ended up too wet for her to wear, and he knew she didn't have a change of clothes.

"Sorry, sweetheart. We can't take a chance on lighting a fire. Climb inside the bedroll out of the wind. That should help some."

Hoping the sand beneath the bedroll still held a little of the heat from today's sun, he helped her snuggle down into it. Then he turned to tug off his own clothes, spreading both his and hers across small boulders nearby. It shouldn't take long for the material to dry in the desert air.

Easing down, he knelt beside her while gently moving a few strands of hair that lay against her cheek. "Better?"

Without opening her eyes, she stuttered, "S-some. B-but still c-cold."

Her sleeping bag had bitten the dust last night as she'd used it to drag him along the rocks. And he didn't have an extra blanket or dry clothes to give her added warmth.

It was impossible for him to stand there and watch her shiver. He couldn't stand seeing her suffer. Sliding himself down into the bedroll beside her, he ignored the tight fit and spooned her close against his chest. If he could've opened up his body and let her crawl right inside, he would've done so without a second thought.

"G-good." She inched her bottom backward, closer still.

Fusing their bodies, he hugged her tightly to him, hoping their combined body heat would warm her eventually.

"N-nice. Thanks." He felt her shuddering in every part of his body—and it drove him near the edge.

"Think nothing of it."

He wasn't sure if those words were meant as a remark to Morgan or to his own libido. Even icy cold, her skin felt as soft as a bunny's fur. Grinning in the dark, he told himself not to think of the sweet, pink panties. Or the way her nipples had peaked against the material of her bra in the cold.

"Try to sleep," he said.

But he didn't expect to get much sleep himself. Not when the most exotic and erotic woman he'd ever seen was snuggled up beside him.

Placing a kiss against her hair, he tried to close his eyes. He'd never been this affected by a woman. She was all he could think about.

He worked hard to force his mind on their mission. On keeping her warm and safe. Not on the way touching her skin made his body harden, yearning for more. But his efforts weren't much use.

He'd been right when he'd thought she was special during training. He just hadn't realized how special. What other woman would be able to survive all that she'd survived and still insist on finishing what they'd started?

The woman was a survivor. She endured.

And now it was his job to endure holding her close but making no advances through the endless hours until morning.

Morgan awoke with a start, not sure why she couldn't move. But the idea of being confined didn't make her afraid. No, this was a good feeling. Cozy. Warm. Like floating on a heated cloud.

Blinking open her eyes at the thought of heat, she looked up to a full moon, riding in a blanket of twinkling stars. The desert. The water. Oh, yeah. But she was deliciously warm now, she thought, as she drifted easily out of her sleep.

Wiggling her toes, she began an inventory. Everything had been numb before, but now she could feel her feet. Her ankles and legs. The next mental stop up her body halted her thoughts and made clear the reason she couldn't move. A heavy, thick leg was thrown over her hip, holding her in place.

Karim. Protecting her. Warming her in his embrace.

Wiggling a hand free, she stroked down his leg, loving the rough texture of his coarse hair against her fingers. The sound of a throat clearing from behind her was her first clue that he was awake.

Her second clue was feeling his rock-hard erection pressing against the small of her back. The pressure grew insistent, yet he made no move to do anything about it. He said nothing, but she could feel his warm breath on her shoulder, tantalizing and seducing.

She wasn't used to anyone protecting her without asking something in return. Suddenly, her normal boundaries dropped away and she knew what she wanted. She wanted to feel alive. Needed to capture his life force and make it her own.

Worming out of his tight hold, she flipped around so she could look at him—touch him. His eyes were open and he gazed at her as if she were the most priceless object he had ever seen.

When her mouth closed over his, he was way ahead of her, taking and giving. He sucked her breath into himself, then fed his back to her. Sharing life.

It was as if he'd known exactly what she'd needed the most.

Their kiss turned to fire, but sweeter, then hotter. His hands were everywhere at once, touching, kneading, caressing. Hers tunneled into his hair, raced up and down his chest. It was as if two starving shipwreck survivors had been able to see the food for days but hadn't been able to reach it. Releasing all that pent-up desire made them greedy. With no words, no permissions or sweet talk, they clawed at each other.

As their tongues dueled and clashed, Karim shoved at her bra, broke the clasp and pushed the whole thing out of his way. Then his mouth clamped on to her nipple. He wasn't the least bit rough, but she wouldn't have minded. Laving and sucking, he drove her to a fever pitch.

Sweat trickled down her neck while heat pooled between her legs. Groaning, she used a free hand to wiggle out of her panties. She wanted nothing in the way. Not clothes nor inhibitions. Nothing.

With the last barrier gone, his fingers tangled in the curls at the apex of her thighs. Not close enough for what she needed. Desperate, she gasped and squirmed, finally bringing her own hand down to move his exactly where she wanted it.

He growled low in his throat, and the sound brushed against

her skin, throbbed in her belly. His fingers did amazing things, made her weep with pleasure, squirm with pure bliss as she rocked against his palm.

She clutched at his shoulders as he suddenly twisted her under him, parted her thighs and positioned his wet tip at her opening. Her heart was thundering in her chest as she whimpered and arched her back, begging him, luring him.

Right at the brink of some amazing discovery when his length nudged her entrance, she dug her nails into his buttocks and pulled him closer. She got what she wanted as he thrust inside. The exquisite awareness—the tremors, the feeling of being filled with heat and pleasure all at the same time—made her dizzy.

He pushed deeper, hesitated. She could feel him right at the border of his control. Without giving her fair warning, a wave rolled through her. Took her right to a cliff, held her there, momentarily suspended over a waterfall of need.

Karim gave one more push, and she washed over the edge on a shower of crazy sensations. Fourth of July fireworks on a sea of exhilaration.

While she sobbed and shouted, Karim moved one final time, following her over. Groaning and shuddering above her, he wrapped his arms around her and held on tight.

So *this* was why she'd been so caught up in him. *This* was the reason people talked about sex making them feel complete. It didn't make them subservient at all. It gave them power.

Ohmygod. She'd never realized. She hadn't known.

Chapter 8

It was dawn when Karim opened his eyes to a slash of sunlight across his face. The mission called to him. Time to move out. Still tangled with Morgan, he carefully slid his arm from beneath her head. She stirred, buried her nose in his shoulder and made a soft noise of protest. Then she rolled over and curled into a ball.

He had little trouble climbing out of the coverings without disturbing her as his sleeping bag was in tatters after their night of lovemaking. The two of them were unbelievably hard on sleeping bags. Good thing they would be completing the mission today and heading home.

Getting to his feet, he stopped to gaze down at Morgan. She made such a picture. All soft and open. What he wouldn't give for an entire night of uninterrupted hours with her and with nothing more pressing than finding all her sweet spots on his agenda.

That would not be today. He turned but couldn't resist one

last glance. Needing to keep an image of her just this way, to hold on forever to what they'd done together, he tried to burn the memory of how she looked into his mind. But what a surprise he got when he discovered that her image was already solidly imprinted inside his heart and locked up tight. So soon?

It seemed he would never forget Morgan or what they'd done. Just how she had been with him. Last night, he'd had the idea that she'd reached a goal she had never touched with anyone else. She was no virgin, but his gut told him she'd never come for any other man. Could that be possible?

It turned out that she was the excitement he'd been trying most of his life to capture, all wrapped up in satin skin and pink panties.

And…she was more. She meant something so much bigger, grander, but what?

Shaking his head, he forced himself to turn away and went for the SAT phone. Too many questions about a woman he was only supposed to protect. Time was running out. If they were to rescue the boy, it had to be today. By tomorrow, his captor would be making good on his ultimatum:

Free the Taj elder in captivity or the Kadir child would die.

But it wasn't good news that Karim received after reaching the team. Zabbarán had broken out in full-scale civil war. Their original plans had to be scrapped. The remaining members of the mission's field team had not been able to find a way into the isolated desert past the many units of Taj Zabbar government soldiers. And any escape attempt by air was out. It seemed the Taj had called upon their Russian friends to supply air support and troops enough to shoot down anything that flew.

But the Kadirs still had their friends and operatives inside Zabbarán. And Karim learned the team had devised a new strategy. He and Morgan were to continue on alone to Nabil Talal's fortress today. But at that point, they would meet up with a group of rebels who had volunteered to help save the boy.

After Morgan did her job, after they'd rescued the child and then escaped capture at the fortress, a Kadir field team would meet them at the nearby port city of Sadutān with a boat. If all went as planned, they would be on their way home by tomorrow.

Karim gently shook Morgan's shoulder. "It's morning. Wake up, Sleeping Beauty. Sorry to awaken you so early but we need to get moving. Want some breakfast before we leave?"

She sat up, stretching like a cat as she shoved her hair away from her face. Her naked body seemed to cause her no concern. But while stretching out the kinks, she made purring noises deep in her throat. Here was yet another memorable picture he wanted for all time.

"Morning," he said again with a hoarse rasp.

He handed over her dry clothes and hoped she would cover up quickly. It was nearly unbearable having to watch and not reach for her.

"Morning. I guess you're trying to tell me it's time to go."

Glad she hadn't said anything about their night together, he went about retrieving something from his pack for her to eat. It wasn't that he didn't wish to talk over what they'd done. But he needed time to straighten out his head.

While he fed her one of the U.S. Army's prepackaged MREs—Meals Ready to Eat—Karim explained the latest plan. Not long afterward, without saying a word, she went to work, checking her rifle and reassembling her backpack.

As she worked she grew quieter. Too quiet. And every time she glanced up, it was with a cold, hard gaze that softened only when she looked his way. He didn't have enough experience with this kind of thing, this mission to murder a madman, for him to account for why she needed the silence. But he wanted to do something to help her.

As he tried to unscramble his own thinking, he thought of what might help give both of them the breathing room they needed. Talking about their pasts and telling each other a little about themselves could work to relax her. And it was infinitely better in his opinion than discussing either their mission or, God help him, last night.

He would rather she did the talking, but he wasn't sure how to get her started. So, he'd have to be the one to spill his guts. His background was a safe and rather boring topic anyway. Nothing much there to upset her or to work against him.

"Mind if I talk while I tear down the camp and load up?" he asked to break the silence.

She shook her head, but she kept her chin down, concentrating on checking her rifle.

He set about cleaning and reloading his own weapons, hoping he wouldn't need to use them again. "I don't know what kind of family you come from…"

Hell, that was no way to start a conversation about himself. Start over.

"I was just thinking about my brother," he began again. "About how he always took such good care of his weapons. He taught me to respect knives and guns and what they can do if you treat them well. I know most of what I know because of him."

"Where is your brother?"

Karim should've known that question would come up. But the deep, aching pain in his chest when it had surprised the devil out of him.

He couldn't make himself say the hated words outright.

Hadn't been able to since it had happened over fifteen years earlier.

"My brother was special," he said instead. "Five years older than me. He was like a superhero in my limited world of books and computers. I thought he could do no wrong. A star athlete, a decent scholar and the most popular boy in school. I idolized him. I wanted to be just like him, but I could never come close."

"Was? You said he *was* special. What happened?"

"Hakim was an adventurer. I once heard a friend of his calling him a power and speed addict behind his back. He was that, all right. Always wanting to climb the tallest mountains, lift the heaviest weights and swim farther than anyone else. His dream as a child was to fly faster than the speed of sound. Faster than anyone else."

Karim had to clear his throat to go on. "He went to work for a U.S. aircraft manufacturer, flight-testing new planes for the Pentagon. On one trip his test plane accidently wandered into North Korea's territory. They shot down his craft without so much as a warning."

"He didn't have an escape pod? A parachute?"

"Yes, of course he had such things. We were never told whether he died from the crash or from a spray of bullets or in a prison camp. His body was never returned. Only his personal effects. Matters of state became too complicated."

Sympathy showed in Morgan's eyes. But she said nothing. He felt her respect for his pain in her silence, and it touched him.

In one way Karim was glad he'd told her the story of his brother. In another way, he wished he'd never started the whole thing.

"Almost ready?" he asked as he shrugged into his pack. "We need to get going if we're to stay on schedule."

She nodded, turning toward the horses. But then she hesitated, turned back and took his hand.

"I had a great time last night, Karim. You've helped me stop thinking for a little while, and I'm really grateful we're on this mission together. Thank you."

Speechless, he dropped her hand and led the way.

Using the GPS and the new coordinates they'd gotten from the Kadir team, they rode through the desert in broad daylight. Karim had turned as silent as she'd been this morning. He was acting as their scout today, glancing periodically through his binoculars for any Taj soldiers. Still, he seemed awfully quiet for someone usually so eager to talk and joke. Morgan supposed both of them needed a little space with their thoughts.

Unlike any of her past missions, this time she couldn't concentrate on the plan, on going over every move in her head on the day of the rescue. Their plans had changed so many times, she would have to go at this one blind. Never a good idea, but something she hoped she could pull off.

As she tried formulating a new mental picture of the moves necessary to make the shot, she discovered all she could think of was Karim. Of what they'd done—and what he'd said.

He had given her the best night of her life. Never before had anyone been so thoughtful, so concerned about her wishes and welfare. In fact compared to the last time… Well, she'd promised herself never to think of that again.

What she and Karim had done was as close to lovemaking as she supposed she would ever have. Certainly closer than her one other time.… Despite her admonitions to the contrary, the memory came back to haunt her. That horrible night in college when she'd been forced could be called a lot of things but never lovemaking. In fact, her experience was more along the lines of what a psychologist had called date rape. Only Morgan knew it shouldn't be called anything quite so polite.

She hadn't led on her date the way he later claimed. In fact, she'd been a virgin and had planned on staying that way until marriage. He, on the other hand, had secretly wanted to prove he was stronger, more athletic and had bigger muscles than the state rifle champion. And the way he went about proving it was to beat her into submission before he did whatever he pleased. In front of two of his buddies.

"You're not so much now. Are you, Miss All-State Champ?" he'd gloated as she'd lain there bleeding and whimpering.

Shaking her head to rid her mind of the memories, she refused the intruding thoughts. Being able to forget that night was imperative for her survival. And what Karim had given her last night was the best memory-eraser in the world.

She thought back on how that miracle had happened. What was so different? She thought she knew. As their mission had gone on, Karim had made her feel comfortable. Highly unusual for a woman in a profession such as hers. In fact, she'd become more than comfortable, really. He'd led her into their relationship gently and made her trust him.

Trust.

He gave her something so different. So incredibly different from anything she had ever known that she would have those new memories to keep her grounded for the rest of her life.

At the thought of the rest of her life, she lifted her head to see what Karim was doing. Suddenly she could dream. And had a new reason to wish. And Karim had done all that by being the one man she could trust implicitly.

As she watched him ride, she realized he also seemed to have grown more comfortable on this mission. At least he'd grown more comfortable astride a horse. He looked magnificent this morning, dashing through the brilliant desert sunlight. His handsome Arabian stallion galloped and pranced, but Karim kept his seat, riding as though he'd been doing it forever.

She opened her mouth to tell him so, to give him encouragement. But then she swallowed down whatever compliment she would've shared. It suddenly seemed too…intimate.

A charge of excitement surrounded Karim. If she tried to make more of their relationship and become closer than ever, he would be a constant temptation. Soon, right after their mission was complete, they would be going separate ways. He off to his wars and adrenaline rushes, and her to a new quiet life. A life she hoped would contain a home and a family.

She now knew she would miss Karim terribly. Being around him was like stepping into a cozy, sexy tornado. It had been the most exciting time of her life. But as with any Fourth of July sparkler, her fingers could so easily be burned.

She swung her attention back to their mission. They weren't far off their original route. With Karim in the lead, the horses strode proudly down a small embankment and entered what the map had called a *wadi:* a valley with a dry river bed, graveled and surrounded by pure sand hills.

Barren and as void of everything as any of the land they'd left behind, the valley seemed stark. Or perhaps, in its own way, this place had a ghostly beauty. Certainly, it was dramatic here. And deadly.

As rare as water was in the Zabbarán land, water had obviously been the sculptor of this valley. She wondered if, on occasion, the water came roaring down from the mountains to flood the plain.

Probably. Their survival training had taught her that flash floods were a distinct possibility in any dry river bed. But not today. The sun shone against the rocks, making them sparkle like diamonds.

Her survival trainers had also cautioned that *wadis* tended to have subsurface water, making them associated with centers of human population in the desert. And she knew this one did just that. According to their map, this *wadi* led to the tiny village situated right below Nabil Talal's fortress.

They were on the last leg of their journey.

For no reason, the hair on her arms stood straight out. Once again, someone was watching. Searching the area ahead, Morgan spotted a flash of light reflected off a glass in the sunshine. A rifle or a pair of binoculars?

Not again. The last time Karim spotted such a sign it had not ended well. Not at all.

Chapter 9

"Karim, look!"

He heard the edge of panic in Morgan's voice, but there wasn't much he could do to soothe her fears. "I see it."

In fact, he'd been noticing many signs of their unseen watchers from almost the first moment they'd entered the *wadi*. "They can't be Taj soldiers. Must be the rebels."

Taj soldiers would've killed them or taken them captive on sight.

"I thought..."

A handful of horsemen appeared over the sand ridge at that moment and started downhill, heading in their direction. Karim halted his horse and indicated that Morgan should do the same with hers.

"You thought we were supposed to meet them right outside of the town at the date palm grove?" He deliberately kept his tone cool to keep her calm. "Yeah, we were. But it looks like they're early."

Morgan took a deep breath, though she remained silent. He wished… But it was too late to talk to her or give her last-minute instructions that might save her life. He had no alternative now except to stay in the saddle and hope that these rebels were the ones they were supposed to meet.

The man on the lead horse came to a halt beside him. "You are the Kadir?" he asked in Taj. The fellow had spit out the words as though disgusted by the idea, and Karim hoped to hell these guys were friendly.

"Yes. Karim Kadir. And…"

"You will come with us." The rebel cut him off before he could mention Morgan's name. "Nabil Talal has his troops hidden along the *wadi,* expecting a rescue attempt of the child. But he is too confident in his forces. We know of a way."

Karim turned and translated for Morgan. She nodded her understanding and acceptance. Then she worked to bring her uneasy horse under control and fall into line with the rebels' horses.

Following the armed rebels, they made their way across the desert until they entered a ravine. One of the rebels rode along the top of the ridge as a sentry, while the rest of them followed the rebel leader into the deep, narrow gorge.

Karim noticed Morgan checking her GPS and saw the worry lines grow across her forehead. He could tell by instinct and the position of the sun that they weren't heading in the direction of Nabil's fortress. Still, they'd run out of options.

When they rode up out of the ravine, they found themselves at the edge of another oasis. The rebel leader indicated they should make no sound. He dismounted and nodded that they were to do the same.

Once off his horse, Karim discovered what the rebels had in mind. A veiled woman driver and her horse-drawn cart filled with hay awaited them behind the tall reeds. He and Morgan climbed in the back of the cart and soon they and their packs were covered with straw.

Karim worried for a second that he might sneeze, but the urge passed as the cart began moving. It was a long, uncomfortable trip, and he wished he could've made it easier on Morgan somehow.

After the cart came to a stop, the woman shoved the straw away and motioned for them to climb out. They stood on flat ground behind a row of ancient-looking, two-story apartments. A couple of the rebels stood watch as they went inside.

"Where are we?" Karim asked the rebel leader once they'd entered the tiny hovel.

"The house of a friend. Follow me."

Following the man, they climbed a narrow set of dark stairs until he shoved at a wooden door. The door creaked open to a space almost too small for Karim to worm through. Then another door opened to the outside.

Karim led the way out onto an empty, flat roof. When he and Morgan looked around, they were surrounded by dozens of rooftops. All empty, save for a few with laundry hanging on makeshift lines and blowing in the breezes.

In the distance, maybe three or four hundred yards away, a castle loomed, situated on a terraced hillside. He spotted lots of rooms and turrets and balconies from this angle. On a second look, Karim decided the place resembled an expensive villa rather than a fortress. A well-fortified villa.

Turning to Morgan, he said, "The shot is too far."

She put her hand on his arm and spoke for the first time since they'd met the rebels. "No. It'll be fine." Her face was a mask, filled with resolute calm again. "I need more information on Nabil's movements."

Karim translated while Morgan asked some pertinent questions. Then it was his turn. He interrogated the rebel to see if there were trusted men who could rescue the child while Karim stayed behind to watch over Morgan. He refused to leave her on her own. And he didn't trust anyone else to be her bodyguard. The rebel leader agreed he would have a small unit stationed nearby to pull the boy out of the fortress after Nabil was dead. It seemed the rebels were willing to risk all for the death of their nemesis.

Karim made final arrangements with the rebel for their escape from town. When he felt as sure about the new plans as he could, he explained everything to Morgan.

"Why don't you go for the boy?" she asked.

Shaking his head, he whispered, "I intend to be here to watch your back so you can feel free to concentrate on the shot. Don't worry. It'll work out. Trust me."

Her eyes lit up with a smile, though her lips never even twitched. "All right, then. The mission is the most important thing. Clear everyone off the roof. I don't want any undue attention drawn to what's happening up here."

The rebels set up a seemingly innocent-looking blind for Morgan before they went back down the stairs. At last alone with her, Karim stood half in and half out of the doorway, watching as she arranged herself underneath a tangle of laundry hanging on a line above her prone body.

Twenty minutes later she lay as still as stone, full concentration dedicated to the fortress in the distance. She'd been through a punishing few days, but no one would ever know it. She must be exhausted, he thought. But there was no way for him to give her aid.

This was her mission now. Her shot. All he could do was stand by her side and think of the young life not four football fields away, awaiting rescue. A young life too precious to lose.

He found himself dwelling on the immobile woman lying nearby with the rifle in her arms. As he thought of her, and as the minutes dragged by in the punishing sun, Karim came to a startling conclusion.

He'd fallen in love—with a sniper.

Morgan felt a trickle of sweat roll down her neck. A fly buzzed her nose. She did not move. Not one muscle.

She dismissed the irritations. It had been hours. Hours in the merciless sun, her attention riveted on her target in the distance.

As the day crept on, she'd studied the lay of the land and the wind currents and waited for Nabil's movements. The flight of a bullet was no mystery to her. In her mind she could clearly see the physics of the trajectory.

So Nabil was the new part of the equation. Nearly every hour on the hour, the bastard kidnapper stepped outside to one of the terraces for a cigarette. Apparently a creature of habits. And a man whose mother had no doubt declared her house off-limits to smoke.

The arrogant son of a bitch had taken no precautions that Morgan could see. He must believe himself to be invincible. His only concession to security was in bringing the child with him outside into the sunshine. As though a baby could be an adequate shield against one of her bullets.

Creep. Coward.

Guardedly, she rolled her shoulders, making sure none of her muscles had gone numb from inactivity. The late-afternoon light had begun to wane. Time was not on her side.

Setting the stock against her shoulder, she checked the sights one last time. Almost the hour for Nabil's indulgence.

Come on, you bastard. You are mine.

A half hour passed. Then fifteen minutes more. She never blinked. Her throat was dry, her muscles screamed.

Morgan felt the sizzle of tension clear to her toes as the first hint of dusk tinged the indigo sky. Then, at last, her quarry stepped into her sights.

Her shot shattered the stillness of twilight. The job was finished.

She felt no pride. No happiness. Only relief that in her lifetime she would never have to take such a shot again. She set aside her rifle, not sure if she ever wanted to pick it up.

Turning, she looked for Karim in the doorway. But he wasn't there.

The shock of seeing an empty space where she had expected to see Karim punched her in the belly. What had happened? He'd been so determined to be her guard. So sure of himself.

He'd told her to trust him.

Grabbing her rifle, she headed for the stairs and some answers. By the time she reached the first floor, she knew she was alone in the house and could hear a commotion outside. Orders were being shouted out in rough voices. Then shots fired and explosions in the distance.

Karim. Did he need her help?

Before she thoughtlessly raced through the front door to find him, she threw a quick, careful glance out the window. In the street outside, rebels fought hand-to-hand with Taj soldiers. The whole town seemed in chaos. She turned and headed out the way she'd entered. Through the back door. But the cart was missing. Their escape route had been blocked.

Dammit, Karim. Where are you?

A Taj soldier suddenly appeared on horseback from around the farthest apartment wall. His steed bore down on her at a gallop, nostrils flaring. The soldier's rifle was fixed with a bayonet and pointed at her.

Bending on one knee, she took aim and fired. The soldier slumped, rolled and landed in a heap on the ground.

Morgan raced toward the riderless horse, swung herself into the saddle and headed off. She no longer had her pack, but she still had her GPS unit. And she had the coordinates to the meeting place for the Kadir rescue party.

She could make it there on her own and hoped that Karim and the child would be waiting. Unless everything that Karim had told her was a lie.

As she rode off alone into the desert under the waning moon, Morgan experienced a couple of things she hadn't felt in too many years to count. Fear. For Karim.

And a single tear, dripping all her hurt and loneliness from the corner of one eye.

Karim pressed Baby Matin's head to his shoulder and followed the rebel leader through the burning alleyways of town. All hell had broken loose the moment that Nabil died. The rebels used their opportunity to begin a surprise attack against the Taj soldiers.

Smoke and the smell of gunpowder soiled the air. Explosions to his left. Machine gun fire to his right.

All Karim could think about was getting back to Morgan. He never should've left her. But when one of the rebels came running up the stairs to say that the baby's rescue team had been captured, he remembered that she had said the mission was all-important. And the mission was rescuing the baby.

His only option was to demand that the rebel messenger stay and guard Morgan while he went for the child. That had been all he could think of to do. And now if he found that the rebel had not done his job and guarded Morgan with his life, Karim would find the man and kill him himself.

The screams of terrified citizens sifted through the horrendous noises made by the rebel leader's AK-47 and broke into his thoughts of Morgan. The rebel sprayed bullets in an attempt to forge a path to lead them back to the apartment. This sudden rebellion was a major screwup in their original plans. Karim had a feeling Morgan would be furious when he reached her.

He had to reach her.

Running through throngs of panicked people, he stayed close behind the rebel leader. Finally, Karim recognized the street corner that led to the row of apartments where Morgan was waiting. He took his first real breath since he'd left.

Until… He turned the corner and saw his worst nightmare. The whole block was on fire. Smoke steamed from every window and many of the roofs had already collapsed in on themselves.

No!

Still not ready to concede the worst, he ran on through heavy smoke to reach the right apartment building, clutching a crying Matin to his chest. The rebel leader stopped, held up his hand as he bent to check on a body lying in the street.

After the rebel leader turned the body over, Karim realized the dead man was the messenger he'd left to guard Morgan. With his heart pounding a staccato beat in his chest, Karim turned to face the apartment now fully engulfed in flames.

Nausea nearly sent him to his knees. Holding Matin in his arms, Karim was plagued by frustration. His inability to do anything about the dire situation unfolding in front of his eyes nearly sent him over an edge. He couldn't race into the burning building to see if Morgan was still there with a baby in his care. He couldn't use his weapon to find a witness to tell him if she'd been taken away by soldiers or—worse—if she had been executed on the spot, her body left to burn.

"We must go." The rebel leader put his hand on Karim's shoulder. "You fulfilled your part of the bargain. The devil Nabil Talal is dead. I will honor my part and save the child. But we must go now."

Karim's stomach rolled and his eyes burned. Could he leave here not knowing what had happened to Morgan?

Just then Baby Matin began coughing, gasping for air as smoke clogged his nose and entered his small lungs. The mission. Morgan's words came back to him: *The mission is the most important thing.*

"All right," he told the rebel. "Lead us out."

As they made their way to the desert, heading for their waiting horses and the fresh air, Karim's eyes clouded, blurring and burning with unshed tears. This was not over for him. He would never rest, never take another easy breath until he found out what had become of Morgan.

He hadn't thought of himself as the type to find love. Long ago he'd become convinced that he would forever be just a lonely tech geek with nothing but computers and machines to take the place of friends and family. That was one of the main reasons he'd decided to assuage his feelings of inadequacy and try to avenge his father's death by imitating his brother and going into the field for missions.

And look how well that had turned out.

He'd left her. Lost her. After giving his word.

The pain of his new loss, of the stinging guilt, stuck in his chest and in his throat, making him crazy. Because of his promise to Morgan, he would save the boy.

But even if it took an army of militia armed with nuclear weapons to get him inside the country again, he would be back.

Chapter 10

Shaking from the cold and worried she was too late, Morgan pulled her horse up a little short of the abandoned well site where everyone was supposed to gather. Now what?

If neither Karim nor any one of the Kadirs were here waiting for her, what could she do? She didn't speak the language and wouldn't know a rebel from a loyalist soldier.

She tethered the horse at a boulder and hefted her rifle, wishing she still had her NVGs. The brilliant stars and the waning moon had gotten her across the desert. But now the goggles or perhaps a flashlight would be truly helpful.

Tiptoeing across the sand, she inched toward the palm trees where she was sure the others should be waiting. But as she rounded a stand of date palms and looked up, she was stunned to find herself surrounded by a group of men wearing heavy, woolen scarves across their faces.

Her heart stopped. Tremors ripped through her limbs. It was all she could do to stand tall and await her fate.

One of the men made a demand in a language she didn't understand. But his meaning seemed clear enough.

She raised her hands above her head. "What do you want?"

"Miss Morgan Bell?" The man spoke in English and his voice sounded familiar, though it was muffled by the material.

He turned and said something to his comrades, then he removed the scarf from his face. "Do you not remember me?"

"Sheik Kalil!" She lowered her arms and started breathing again.

"You would do me a great favor, Miss Bell, if you would give me your weapon—temporarily, of course. The sight of a woman with a rifle worries the men."

Gladly. Morgan wouldn't need this gun from here out, and she never wanted to see a sniper's rifle again.

She raised her arm slowly and handed it over to the sheik. "Please accept the rifle with my compliments and gratitude. I gift it to you with all my thanks."

The sheik nodded, then said, "You are early, Miss Bell. We await the Kadir and the Kadir child. I understand they have escaped some small trouble."

So, she hadn't been too late and already missed Karim and the others. Thank God. She wanted to know what kind of trouble they'd had but could not seem ungrateful enough to question the sheik.

"I...uh...didn't know you were planning to help us leave the country, Sheik Kalil. I'm surprised to see you."

"All those who wish for freedom in the country of Zabbarán are willing to help the Kadirs. But secreting a Kadir child out of the country will not be so easy."

Sheik Kalil crossed his arms over his chest and slowly shook his head as he continued, "Every Taj soldier in the land is looking for this boy and the men who killed Nabil. A bounty has been issued for your heads. The rebels have called upon bedouins to assist in the effort to see your team safely away."

A chill ran down the back of her neck. She'd never had a bounty on her head before. And the baby? What kind of people wanted the head of an innocent child for revenge?

This whole mission had turned to chaos. She would have a lot to say to Tarik Kadir for getting her into this mess.

But her thoughts suddenly turned to a different Kadir, not Tarik. She wasn't sure what she would say to Karim when he finally arrived. They would have to rely on each other to get themselves and the boy out of Zabbarán. But could she ever really trust him again?

"Come," Sheik Kalil said quietly. "Take water and refresh while we await your companions. It may be a long night."

If Karim hadn't had Baby Matin tied in a sling at his chest, he would have fallen to the ground with relief when he first saw Morgan with the bedouins. Tongue-tied, he went to her and touched her cheek, assuring himself that she was really there. Really okay.

"H-how…?" He couldn't get the words out. What he wanted to say must stay locked up inside until another time when they were finally safe and alone.

"We have a lot to talk about," she said coldly. "Later. Right now I need to see that the baby is all right."

She held out her arms and waited for him to loosen the sling around his neck and turn Matin over to her care. The baby seemed grateful to be free. He nearly flew into Morgan's arms.

The minute she had a good hold on the child, her face—her whole body—softened. It was an amazing transformation. Like magic.

Matin must've noticed it, too. With tiny, chubby fingers, he patted her cheek as he'd seen Karim do. "Mama."

Morgan threw a dark glance over at Karim, then riveted her attention back on the boy.

"You're going to be all right, Baby," she murmured. "I won't let anything happen to you. I give you my word."

She said the last with emphasis, and made Karim wonder if the comment was really meant for him. It had sounded like a rebuke.

"If Matin doesn't believe that, I can vouch for your word." Emotion hitched in his voice, and he felt himself on a tenuous thread.

He wanted badly to talk to her. To explain why he'd left her alone. To tell her that he never wanted to leave her again. But this certainly wasn't the time or the place.

Morgan stopped fussing over the child for the moment and put her hand on Karim's arm. "Don't say things like that. You don't really know me."

"Yes, I do. I know you like order and stability. And I know you're a survivor. I also know you have a tender heart underneath the cold, tough façade." He bent, feathering a whisper-soft kiss on her lips. "I wish…" His voice utterly abandoned him.

"Nice family picture." Sheik Kalil came over and stood in the shadows of the moon. "But we must move. We're on a timetable. Your arrival at the new meeting spot at the port is expected before high tide."

Karim gathered up Morgan and the baby and shuffled them toward a waiting Jeep. With his arm around her shoulders, he noted that she seemed fragile under her thin garments. Not at all like her usual cold-as-steel tenacity.

As Morgan took the child and climbed into the back of the open Jeep, he shrugged out of his pack and jacket. Then he placed the heavy coat over her shoulders, wrapping it around both her and Matin, whom she held in her arms. He knew she wouldn't give in and rest until the baby was safe. But he also saw the strain in her eyes. Her world had shifted. Her well-drawn plans had crumbled.

And he could do nothing more for her than give her support.

Hours later the three of them sat huddled in a fishing shack, waiting to be picked up by a trawler. Morgan sat next to him on the floor with her head resting on his shoulder. Karim had tried to get her to eat something or to take a nap, but she seemed much more concerned about the child than her own welfare.

Earlier, she'd asked him to beg one of the rebels, who'd traveled along with them to act as their guards, to find a soft cloth for use as a diaper and some bread for the baby to eat. Now dry and warm with a full tummy, the little boy lay snoozing against her chest.

Karim's own chest ached with wanting to protect these two. To shelter them from any further harm and keep them safe—for good. He'd never experienced feelings like these before. All his life he'd had no one who'd depended on him. First his older brother and then his father had made sure his happy, little, isolated world was secure. He'd always had them around as protectors.

Looking down at the two people in his arms, Karim felt his old perceptions shattering and new ones taking their place.

A noise broke into his thoughts as he heard the rebels talking quietly right outside the shack. It must be time to go. The trawler they were supposed to board needed the high tide to motor beyond the reef. Once they'd made it past the harbor, one of the Kadir family's ships would be waiting to pick them up about twenty miles offshore.

Karim looked forward to having a day or two aboard a

large ship to talk to Morgan as they cruised back to safety. He felt sure he could make her see that they belonged together. Though he wasn't positive how the two of them would make that happen in practicality. She wanted the peace and quiet of her Wyoming ranch. He couldn't imagine leaving his Kadir cousins and their war with the Taj.

"It's time." One of the rebels stuck his head in the doorway. The man had changed into the clothes of a Taj fisherman.

Karim roused Morgan and then helped her stand without waking Matin. As they sneaked out the shack's door, the gray-and-lavender light of dawn surprised him. He had assumed they would be using the dark to hide their escape.

"We need to hurry," he urged. He didn't like the feel of the wharf, though everything nearby seemed deserted and quiet.

Hustling to the dock, they slipped into a dinghy, and one of the rebels rowed them out the fifty yards or so to the waiting trawler. An older, wooden boat, the trawler bounced like a bobber on the incoming tide.

When the dinghy arrived at the side of the trawler, Karim could see they would have problems boarding the vessel. A rope ladder was the only method of climbing aboard. How would Morgan make it with Matin in her arms?

"Give me the baby," he told her.

She shook her head. "Go on ahead and then you can help us over the side. I'll manage the ladder."

Looking up the length of the ladder and then checking over his shoulder, he was once again frustrated by not being able to do his job. They were too exposed. But they had no choice.

One of the rebels scrambled up, over the side and into the boat first, while a second man stayed in the dinghy and held the ladder tight. Maybe everything would be all right.

Karim went up as fast as he could. When his feet were on solid deck, he turned and leaned over the side. Morgan was already on her way up. But she was being careful, going slow, trying to keep Matin safe in the crook of one arm while she used the other to climb.

All of a sudden shots rang out from the dock and a bullet whizzed close by his head. They were under attack! And taking rifle fire. The sound of another bullet zinging past caught his attention the hard way. He felt a fiery sting biting into the flesh of his shoulder and knew it had been too close. But it wasn't bad enough for him to flinch or cry out.

"Hurry," he shouted down to Morgan.

He could hear a motorboat starting up back at the dock and knew they would soon be facing Taj soldiers. He had to help Morgan and the child board now.

Hooking his feet on a couple of heavy, wire fish traps, he leaned as far out of the boat as he dared. He heard the trawler's engines starting up beneath decks and felt the motion of the fishing vessel getting under way.

When Morgan was only a couple of feet from the edge, she stopped and planted her feet inside the rope's rungs. "Take the baby."

She shoved the boy above her head and into Karim's waiting arms. He pulled the child against his chest. As the boat rolled he lost his balance, landing hard on his back on the deck. A fisherman took the baby, allowing Karim to help Morgan climb aboard.

Once again Karim braced his feet and leaned over the side. She was close enough now that he could grab her. He latched his arms under her arm pits just as she grabbed hold of his neck.

He tugged as hard as he could—while hearing more shots ringing out through the darkness. They got lucky. Her whole body easily came with him as they fell back over the edge. They'd made it.

"You're safe," he shouted past the noise of the trawler's engine racing away from their pursuers.

But she didn't answer. She didn't move.

"Morgan?" He pulled her up into his arms, but she was as limp as a rag doll.

And then he found the blood. Too much blood. When he rolled her over and spotted bullet holes in her back, his stomach pitched, and a red haze came down over his eyes.

No! It couldn't be so. His brain couldn't process the truth. He refused to accept that he might have just lost the one woman in his life who had made him feel like a whole man.

"You should see him." Tarik Kadir stood beside Morgan's hospital bed in Germany, annoying her with his pleas on behalf of his cousin. "Karim hasn't left the hospital since the moment you were brought in. He's barely slept and I have trouble getting him to eat. One of the surgeons practically threw him in the shower this morning because he'd started to smell so bad.

"See him, dammit, and put me out of my misery."

Still weak but growing stronger by the hour, Morgan figured it was useless to keep refusing to listen to whatever Karim had to say. But she was afraid of her own reactions—of her traitorous heart.

He'd saved her life and the life of the baby. Since she'd come out of surgery, Tarik had told her the whole story. He'd given her the facts of how Karim had raced through horrendous street battles to rescue Matin at the fortress after the rebels had deserted their posts. He hadn't willingly left her.

Tarik also told of how, when they were aboard the trawler, even though he'd been wounded himself, Karim had stood over her and the baby, firing at the pursuing Taj until they'd reached the Kadirs' ship and help. And finally, Tarik made her listen to how Karim had donated his own blood when she'd lost so much the Kadir ship's doctor was afraid she might not last until they could helicopter her to a hospital.

What could she say to a man like that?

"Morgan, he's right outside. Please."

"All right." This discussion would have to come about sooner or later.

In seconds, Karim had taken his cousin's place at her bedside. "How are you feeling?"

She looked up into his eyes and immediately her throat closed. Wanting him so much that she was physically ill with the need, she could barely talk. But she had to keep reminding herself that a relationship between the two of them could never happen. They were too different.

"Better," she finally managed. "How's your arm?"

"It's nothing." He gazed down at her and fisted his hands.

He wanted to touch her, she could tell. She knew him well enough by now. And she wanted that, too. But she didn't reach for him. Instead she started to open her mouth to give the little speech she'd planned but quickly shut it again after really gazing up into his face.

Just look at his expression. That expression clearly said he adored her. That she meant enough for him to give up his life for her.

No one had ever looked at her with such desire and tenderness at the same time. Oh, lordy, her whole body ached for him. Maybe there *could* be a chance for them.

"I…I wanted to say I'm sorry," he said with a hoarse rasp. "I didn't do my job. It was my fault you almost died. On my next mission, I'll do better."

Her heart sank, the tiny flicker of hope she'd harbored disappeared. "You're going out on more missions? I would've thought you'd had enough. You've already avenged your father's death in the best possible way by saving a child's life. You're a good person, Karim. Doesn't a little peace and security sound nice after what we went through?"

His gaze grew even more tender, if that were possible, and his voice lowered to a whisper. "When you say I'm a good person, I can almost believe it. But peace and security can't be any part of my life until the Taj give up their vendetta against our family."

Oh, God. They would never have anything in common.

"The doctors say I'll be released tomorrow or the next day," she said instead of what her heart wanted her to say. "I'm eager to go home."

As his expression darkened, she thought of something they had in common after all. "How's Baby Matin? Where is he? Can I see him before I go back to America?"

"Tarik's brother Shakir and his wife have custody of Matin at their Mediterranean island children's sanctuary. But it's temporary, until the Kadir council can decide which Kadir family should get the baby on a more permanent basis."

The sadness she felt became nearly overwhelming. "Will he be okay?"

"I will make sure the baby is happy and well cared for. You can count on it."

Before she could make another remark, he blurted out, "Come with me, Morgan. Don't go home to your ranch. Make a life with me and help us fight the Taj instead."

Her whole body trembled with need. "I can't. You like jumping off the edge and diving into trouble—sandstorms, civil war. You like the adrenaline of it. But I'm done with that kind of life. I'm planning on building a very different kind of life for myself."

She took a deep breath. "I...just can't."

Karim's eyes grew cloudy as he tilted his head to study her face. "You want the kind of life where I don't belong?"

Morgan didn't know how to answer. The sadness in her

chest grew more insistent at the idea of never seeing him again. But—

"You know," he said slowly. "Sometimes even the best-made plans are destined to be changed."

Shaking her head, she closed her eyes and tried to close her heart. "Not these plans. Not this time."

Chapter 11

Morgan stomped into her late grandmother's kitchen, tired and hungry. And so lonely, she thought, she might die of it.

Nearly two months now since she'd come back to her childhood home in Wyoming, and nothing was like she'd thought it would be. Her second cousins were the ones running the family ranch and using the first floor of this house as an office. She'd been happy to see her extended relatives again and thought if she moved in upstairs, it would be nice having people around all the time.

But that was the trouble. These were just people. Not real family. They didn't love her.

She didn't belong here. This wasn't her place anymore. Besides, she missed Karim so bad sometimes it made her hurt all over. The look of pain on his face when she'd sent him away for good at the hospital still made nightly appearances in her nightmares.

Shaking off the melancholy and going to the sink, she

washed her hands, preparing to make herself some lunch. But instead, she stood there, looking out the kitchen window at the horse corral she'd left a few minutes earlier. She swiped absently at a lone tear and thought, *How silly.*

There wasn't much she could do that was useful here on this enormous ranch. Hired hands did all the fun work like caring for and moving the herds. Her second cousin, Neil, kept the books and took care of all the paperwork. Morgan felt out of place, and she worried all the time how she would ever make a life for herself here—or anywhere.

"Morgan?" Neil swung open the door and stuck his head in the room. "I thought I might find you in the kitchen. There's someone here to see you."

Someone? As in, another person that she didn't care about?

But as she dried her hands and prepared to follow Neil out to the office, the *someone* brushed past her cousin's retreating back and stormed into the room just as the door swung closed behind him.

Now this was someone she did care about. "Karim." What was he doing here?

And how did she look? Where was a mirror when you really needed one?

"I...hope it's okay." His rugged profile, the stubborn chin and deep-set eyes twisted her all around.

"Of course it is. I'm glad to see you. Would you care to sit down?"

She pulled out one of the chairs from around the big kitchen table and gestured for him to take it. "Can I get you something? Coffee? Water? I was just about to make myself some lunch. I could..."

"Please." He took her hand as he sat down. "Sit with me. I have something to say. To ask."

Crazy idiot that she was, she'd been babbling due to a huge case of nerves. Now, as she felt the warmth of his hand holding hers, she couldn't think of a thing to say. So, she sat down in the chair next to his and closed her mouth.

Maybe she was holding her breath, waiting to hear what he had to say. Or maybe she had died, and this was all a dream where she didn't need any air at all.

"First of all," he began, sounding too sharp. "Tarik tells me I am a fool."

She felt Karim's thumb rubbing circles on her palm. The electric sensations he created were making it hard to concentrate on his words, but they went a long way toward calming her down.

"Morgan Bell, do you know that I love you?"

Her breath whooshed out in a rush. "What?" No, wait. That was a stupid thing to say. Think of something else—something better.

"I mean, yes, Karim Kadir. I do know that you love me."

"Well, I never said it before, and Tarik tells me that was not very smart. Women like to hear the words sometimes."

He swallowed hard as he held both her hands and stared into her eyes, his tender gaze making the butterflies in her stomach soar. "I don't expect for you to say you love me back. But the thing is, I believe you do care for me. And if that's true, I wondered if perhaps you would give me the time to make you happy—to show you how much I care."

She opened her mouth to tell him she would give him anything if he would just shut up and kiss her. But before she could, he dropped her hands and stood, nervously pacing the floor next to the table.

"I've learned a lot about me since I last saw you in the hospital," he said. "I found out that I'm much happier working with computers and machinery than I am in the field. I guess I should've known that all along, but I had always wanted so bad to be like my brother that I…"

With a look of frustration, he slammed one of his fists into the other palm. "I suppose you can call me stupid along with foolish. Anyway, I've decided—with Tarik's sincere encouragement—to stay out of the field and go back to helping the Kadirs with their electronic needs."

"Oh?" She still wasn't able to utter anything more than one syllable.

"Yes. And I'm not sure if you understand this, but I can do that kind of work from anywhere in the world. I don't have to necessarily be located at the Kadirs' Mediterranean compound or anywhere close. So…"

He inhaled a deep breath and rushed ahead. "I was hoping you might give me a job. I can handle any kind of machinery or vehicles. Tractors. Hay balers. Trucks. Or I could set up a new computer accounting system for the ranch. Just as long as I can work part-time for the Kadirs, it doesn't—"

"Wait." She held up her hand and stood, too. "You want to move *here?* So the two of us can be together?"

He halted in his tracks. The look of panic that appeared on his face was priceless. He was worried she would say no.

Going to his side, she gently touched his chest. "Listen to me, Karim. I was wrong to insist on coming back here to what I thought of as home. Home can be anywhere. On a schooner on the Indian Ocean. Or in an ice house on the frozen tundra in the Arctic. Or even in the back of an RV rolling down the highway."

He covered her hand on his chest with one of his own. She could see the hope creeping into his expression.

"What makes it home is the love," she continued. "The sense of belonging and the people there who care. I won't give you a job here. But I will go with you—anywhere. As long as we're together, it'll be our home."

That's when he did kiss her. Finally. The warmth, the longing, everything he was feeling combusted inside her like a Molotov cocktail exploding on impact.

As he pulled back for air, he whispered, "Stay with me always, Morgan. Marry me."

She dragged his head down to kiss him again, letting him know she accepted his proposal. They would be together. They would be a family. Always.

High on a breezy hill, with the aquamarine of the Aegean Sea in the distance, Karim Kadir saved his heart. He married the love of his life with his cousins and their families looking on.

Now, the two of them stood arm in arm, watching the others dance. Just happy to be together. So far the day had been one of his best. The weather was clear. The food and songs were his favorites. It was almost perfect.

But he wanted everything. He wanted perfect.

Though he might be a fool, he wasn't stupid. He hadn't given Morgan a chance to change her mind after she'd agreed to marriage. He'd whisked her off to the Kadirs' compound and only gave her a couple of days to prepare. And she seemed happy about it all. But every once in a while he saw a sad look come into her eyes, and he was arrogant enough to believe he knew why.

Placing a quick kiss across her lips, he said, "I have a gift for you."

"Another one?" She laughed and hugged him tighter. "You've already bought me property and a house here on this hill. And made arrangements to bring in riding horses so I can train your cousins how to ride in the desert. What else?"

"Wait." He turned and signaled to Shakir, who'd been waiting for the sign. "Now, close your eyes."

When she did as he asked, Karim hurried over to pick up her present and get back to her side before she opened her eyes or peeked out of curiosity.

"What is it, husband?"

The sound of those words made him ever more eager to please her in any way possible. "Okay. Now you may look."

As she opened her eyes, he saw exactly the emotions he had hoped to see.

"Matin! Oh, Karim. You've brought the baby to our wedding. That's the best present yet. Thank you." She reached out and took the boy who seemed just as happy to see her.

Over babbling baby talk, she gazed lovingly up at Karim. "How long can he stay? Who are his new parents?"

Now was the time to tell her all. "If you agree, *we* are his parents. I spoke to the Kadir council and they think we would be perfect for the job."

He waited, afraid to move. Knowing this was asking a lot of such a planner on short notice, he listened to the beating of his own heart. Warily, he watched as his new wife took in the meaning of her gift.

Suddenly, she burst into tears and clutched the baby closer. Karim had never seen his strong-willed, intense wife cry.

Backpedaling, he desperately sought to find the right thing

to say. "I'm sorry. I know you hadn't planned for this. But I thought—"

"Oh, Karim, I love you so much. We're going to make such a wonderful family." She leaned against his side, and he closed his arms around both her and the baby.

Perfect.

* * * * *

SHEIK'S CAPTIVE

Loreth Anne White

For Linda Conrad, always an inspiration, and to the team at Harlequin, always wonderful to work with.

Chapter 1

Kathleen Flaherty stood at the bedouin tent entrance, her robes fluttering softly about her ankles as she watched darkness descend over the dry, distant Sahara range. The Adrar Plateau lay over those distant mountains. Her guides said they could possibly reach the plateau by tomorrow night. But the going would be rough.

Kathleen didn't care how rough. She just prayed Adrar would yield some clue as to what might have happened to her sister, Jennie, missing for nine months now. The mystical Adrar Plateau was where a bedouin elder said he'd glimpsed a woman resembling the photograph of Jennie that Kathleen had been showing around in Tessalit. It was Kathleen's last hope. If no new information surfaced in Adrar, Jennie's trail would grow cold, and Kathleen would be left with no idea where to turn.

But while her own anxiety had been mounting over what tomorrow might bring, Kathleen had sensed a different kind of tension growing in her guides as they'd neared those mountains. She'd glimpsed it in the flicker of an eye, the quick exchange of a glance, a nervous movement. And she was beginning to feel as if their tiny convoy might be venturing into hostile territory.

The wind, tinged with campfire smoke, gusted a little harder, nosing under flaps, billowing the canvas structure. While it was a change from the airless, blistering temperatures through which Kathleen and her small caravan had traveled throughout the day, the breeze provided scant relief. It remained hot, dry, and in her imagination, the moving air rustled with warnings about an unknown danger lurking somewhere over those mountains. Kathleen tried to shake the notion, but that was her failing—a flair for the dramatic, a wild imagination. And it was *not* coupled with bravado. Kathleen was crap-scared by what she was doing out here.

But it was sheer desperation that had driven her to this point because no one—not the U.S. State Department, FBI, Interpol, the Burkina Faso government nor any other agency—had been able to help Kathleen locate her missing sister, and for nine months she'd badgered them all. Kathleen had actually begun to think she was being stonewalled. So, as a last resort, she'd packed her own bags and headed for Tessalit in northern Mali, from where a postcard had come with a cryptic phrase hastily scrawled in Jennie's distinctive hand, in Gaelic: *Taim i gcruachais anois.*

A cry for help in the language of their ancestors, a language Jennie had taught Kathleen as a child. It was their special, secret oasis of communication in a dysfunctional family with an absent mother and a philandering, alcoholic father.

Kathleen turned to watch her old Berber guide squatting besides the fire he'd built at the center of their camp. He was crouched forward, tending to a blackened pot that hung over the flames. He'd likely sit there all night, stoking the fire until dawn rippled once more over the Sahara.

The younger of her two guides ordinarily kept vigil by the fire with the old man and, from inside her tent, Kathleen would listen to their soft, intermittent, Arabic chatter—a comforting, human sound in the vast and desolate Sahara blackness.

But tonight, the young guide was out in the desert somewhere along the periphery of their camp where the camels had been hobbled so they could chew on sharp tufts of grass sprouting between rock. Kathleen couldn't see him in the darkness, but she could hear the thin notes coming from his flute. She wondered why he'd chosen this particular night to leave the comfort of the fire to guard the camels.

With growing unease, she lowered her tent flap for privacy and lit a candle. The flame guttered in the breeze as she changed into her nightgown, the hot, waxy scent reminiscent of a time past—or so the historian in her imagined. Kathleen loved old things, beautiful things, that took time to craft and were made with passion and care. To her, they represented value, respect, commitment.

Seating herself on her camp cot she reached for the cloth saddlebag at her side and removed a leather-bound journal— her last birthday gift from Jennie. The feel of old leather against her palms grounded Kathleen. But as she opened the cover, Jennie's postcard slipped out, falling to the sand, rattling her all over again.

Kathleen picked the card up—a picture of an oasis on the front, the Gaelic scrawl on the back. There was zero doubt in her mind it had come from Jennie. Her chest tightened as she turned the card over. Jennie was in some kind of deep trouble, and she'd been trying to communicate this to her sister in secret. Why? What was she afraid of?

Where was she now?

How on earth could she have just have vanished without a clue from the medical convention she'd been attending in Burkina Faso to find herself in Tessalit, a small town in northern Mali. It made no sense.

Kathleen tucked the card into the back of her diary and opened the book to a blank page.

She began to write.

We're close to Adrar now, and I must confess I am afraid. I'm not sure whether to be more apprehensive of learning a terrible truth about Jennie, or of finding nothing, my search coming to a dead end. But oddly, under my fear, under the sheer desperation that drove me here, I am learning something about myself. This Sahara desert, its history, its peoples who once lived only in my dreams and between the pages of beloved old tomes, are coming to vivid life. And in a way, so am I. I've been forced out of the pages of my books to physically walk these burning sands myself, to meet and talk to and touch the people that make a home in these desolate plains, and it's awakening something in me...

Her pen stilled.

Kathleen looked up. Was that the chink of a bridle she'd heard?

The wind had fallen silent. The thin, clear notes of the flute had also died. She listened intently for some sound but could hear nothing. Yet she sensed a presence in the air.

Kathleen slowly rose, opened the tent flap. Her guide still sat by the fire, his back to her, his turbaned head bent forward as he poked the logs. Sparks spattered hot orange up into the black sky. It all looked normal. Perhaps the young guide had simply fallen asleep.

She resumed her position and writing.

* * *

Sayeed Ali dismounted, landing soft as a cat in the warm sand. Bandoliers containing rounds of ammunition crisscrossed his chest. A scimitar and dagger were sheathed in leather at his waist. His black tunic, black cotton pants, black boots and black turban that left only slits for his eyes rendered him almost invisible against the darkness.

Moonlight glinted off bridles as the twelve other men in the hunting posse silently circled the camp astride their horses. Similarly swathed, they moved like black blots against the desert night.

Sayeed raised his hand, giving them the signal to wait along the periphery of the camp. Then he crept in a crouch toward the back of the woman's tent, the hilt of his curved dagger warm in his palm.

The guard they'd encountered outside the camp lay still, lifeblood from his carotid draining into thirsty sand, his flute silent in limp fingers. The man had not seen nor heard the mounted posse coming. His fate had been swift, which was a relief to Sayeed.

Creeping closer to Kathleen Flaherty's tent, he aimed for a slit in the canvas through which a strip of yellow light flickered. His orders were clear—locate the American woman's camp, kill her and everyone else traveling with her on sight. Not one witness to be left alive.

Inching the canvas slit open with the backs of his fingers, Sayeed peered through the gap. Shock rippled through him.

His target sat on a camp cot, writing in a book by the light of a candle. She wore a white cotton nightdress—ankle length—with little eyelets along the hem. Old-fashioned but startlingly sexy to Sayeed. Her bare feet were slim with delicate arches, and they rested on a faded woven rug she'd laid over the sand. Hair the color of a red Sahara sunset fell in a thick wave across her cheek as she bent forward. Her skin was like alabaster but, as she hooked a fall of auburn hair behind her ear, Sayeed could see that the desert sun had burned and freckled her nose and cheeks.

She bit her bottom lip as she wrote, and Sayeed noted she was using a fountain pen and that her journal was bound in leather. He'd seen occasional tourists brave this part of the Sahara—usually Germans. Sometimes the odd American. They tended to wear the latest in adventure gear and carry high-tech navigational equipment, but this woman looked like something beautiful and gentle out of a colonial past, and the vignette threw him.

He could see in Kathleen Flaherty the genetic echoes of her older sister. But while Dr. Jennie Flaherty was whippet-thin with angular features and hair more honey-blond than red, this much younger woman had gentle curves, a soft, feminine sexiness that unexpectedly did something to Sayeed. Stalling him. Mesmerizing him. And for a strange moment rendering him immobile, indecisive. And it cost him.

Because, before he could force himself to rip open the canvas and take his quarry, he heard Qasim sound the command.

The Moors came roaring into camp, hooves drumming on hard sand. They shrieked like a band of wild marauders, machetes and scimitars wielded up high as they bore down on the old Berber guide at the campfire.

Adrenaline slammed into Sayeed.

He raced to the front of the tent, yelling at them to stop. But it was too late.

Bloodcurdling screams sliced through the night, and Kathleen gasped, dropped her book, a raw, primal terror clawing through her. She dashed to the tent flap, yanked it open, and her stomach turned to water at the sight before her.

Silhouetted by firelight, men on black horses with scimitars held high were bearing down on her old guide. He screamed for mercy in high-pitched Arabic, arms raised above his head, but they forced him back toward the flames.

One of the men leaned down as he barreled past on his horse and swung his scimitar across the guide's neck. Time turned slow and thick as Kathleen saw the guide's head loll back, a gaping red maw appear across his neck, the spurt of arterial blood.

The old Berber seemed momentarily suspended in midair, then he sank slowly to his knees and slumped to the ground. Flames began to lick at his white robes, sparks fizzing and crackling hot orange in the night.

Bile lurched to her throat. But before she could move, the killer on the horse caught sight of her. She froze. The man's eyes glittered evilly from the slit in his black turban. He pointed his sword at her and yelled in Arabic. Then he kicked his horse and came for her at full gallop, scimitar pointed forward like a knight's lance. The hooves of the other marauders thudded behind him as the men began their wild shrieking again.

Kathleen flung back into her tent, desperately searching for something she could use as a weapon, but the horseman swiped at a support pole and the heavy canvas flopped down on top of her, dropping her to her knees. Ensnared in canvas and guy ropes, Kathleen was dragged through the sand behind the horse, her head hitting rocks, a sharp one gashing her temple.

The killer stopped suddenly, rearing his horse.

Quickly disentangling herself from the canvas, Kathleen got up to run. Her assailant laughed, head thrown back to the stars, then with a wild, ululating shriek, he barreled down on her again, lunging with his sword as he rode past.

Kathleen threw herself to the ground, rolling in a ball as she hit sand. The tip of his scimitar missed its mark, slicing only the fabric down her back and leaving a thin, searing burn across her skin, fine as a razor cut.

With a violent curse her attacker dropped down from his horse and marched toward her.

He grabbed a fistful of her hair, lifting her from the ground so that her toes dangled just above sand. The tearing pain in her scalp was so severe it left no wind in her lungs to scream. He unsheathed his dagger, pressed the blade to her throat.

Kathleen said a silent prayer.

But with a resonating clang, the dagger shot free of her attacker's hand, flying in a wide arc to the sand.

Another tribesman, taller, broader, also dressed all in black, stepped forward.

"This kill," he said in Arabic, "is *mine*."

Chapter 2

"Please," Kathleen whispered, tears filling her eyes so that the man above her blurred into a dark, looming form. "Please don't kill me."

He raised his sword and a scream swelled into her chest. But instead of bringing the blade down on her neck, he sheathed it at his waist.

"My name is Sayeed Ali," he said. In English. Not French. Nor Arabic, nor any of the more common languages spoken in the Sahara. He reached down to help her to her feet, but as he did, the other man lunged at him with his sword.

Her savior ducked to the side, avoiding the swipe of the blade. As he moved, he unsheathed his own curved sword and swung, slicing her attacker's wrist.

The attacker dropped his scimitar and clamped his hand over the bleeding wound. He glared at the man called Sayeed, neck muscles pumped in rage, black eyes crackling in fury.

The other men in the posse dismounted and moved closer,

drawing horses by bridles. Tension hung thick, simmering, silent.

Kathleen tried to scoot back in the sand, but her rescuer stomped his leather boot onto the edge of her nightgown, trapping her like a bug on the dirt.

"Why do you let her live?" Her attacker demanded in an Old Arabic dialect that surprised Kathleen, a dialect she understood with a scholar's passion. "Our orders were to kill her on sight!"

"We will kill her, Qasim. But first we interrogate her." Her savior spoke in Arabic again, calm, a low, guttural, rolling sound.

Horses whinnied as the circle of men drew even closer.

"Interrogate her! Are you stupid? Bakkar said he wants her *dead,* not questioned!" The man called Qasim waved his arm in a wide sweep. "He ordered everyone in this camp dead. And you let our key target live?"

"And you challenged my command of this raid," said Sayeed, his voice very low, but dangerous, subtext lingering heavily. The other men seemed to hang on to each word, observe every nuance of movement—wild and violent marauders watching to see which of these two dominant tribesmen would emerge victorious.

"Bakkar made it clear I was in charge."

"You took too long behind the tent."

"And you made a mistake by not being patient enough to wait for my sign." Sayeed pointed at her on the ground. "This woman might know something. She could have told others. That could lead another search party in this direction. Sheik Bakkar Al Barrah would *not* like that—it could be fatal for our plan. We will take her to the camp, question her there. Bakkar can then decide how he wants to dispose of her."

Kathleen began to shake. They had to have made a mistake. They had the wrong woman.

They'll let me go when they figure it out, surely?

Qasim glared at Sayeed. The other men shuffled. Finally, the attacker reached for his fallen sword, sheathed it. Muttering an explicit curse, he turned and yelled for his horse. "And what are you fools all looking at?" he barked at the other men as he swung himself up onto his tasseled saddle. "Get moving—burn everything in the camp, then clear out!" He kicked his horse and galloped, hooves thundering, into the blackness of the night, dust clouding behind him.

"Search her tent first," ordered Sayeed as he watched his challenger vanish into darkness. "I want this woman's journal and any photos you find. Burn everything else."

Sayeed bent down and clasped Kathleen's hand. His grip was warm, strong, his palm rough. He pulled her to her feet. "Walk," he demanded, pushing her forward. "To my horse over there."

But she was shaking so badly that her legs buckled out from under her. He caught her, hauling her up again, and he held her steady as he marched her forward. His body was hard, hot, the fabric of his tunic rough against the skin on her back where her nightgown had been cut open.

She craned her neck, trying to see what was happening. Men were running from the campfire with sticks ablaze. They set the burning sticks to her tent and belongings. Canvas billowed up in a hot *whoosh*. One of the men ran out ahead of the flames carrying her journal and a box of photos of Jennie.

"No!" She tried to jerk free. "Wait, that's mine! Please, don't—"

Sayeed silenced her with a rough shove from his knee and a yank on her arm. "Quiet," he hissed. "Keep walking. Fight me, try to escape, and maybe I won't be able to save you next time."

He shoved her forward.

Terrible, burning scents and thick, black smoke choked the air. Kathleen thought of her guides, men she'd been responsible for bringing out here, now dead. She was shaking badly—big, body shudders that made her stumble to the ground again. He yanked her up again. Tears rolled down her cheeks. She tried to wipe them from her face, but her hand came away sticky with blood. The wound on her temple was still bleeding badly. Her nightgown was full of her own blood.

Sayeed hauled Kathleen up onto his horse. He positioned her between his thighs on the saddle, and he put his arms around her to take the reins.

"What is your name?" he whispered against her ear.

"Ka…Kathleen Falherty."

"Trust me, Kathleen. Do everything I say, and you might live. Understand?"

"Why?" she pleaded, struggling to turn around and face him, tears filling her eyes. "Why did you do this? What do you want from me? Who *are* you all?"

"Shhh." His breath was warm through her hair, his demeanor almost gentle now that they were momentarily out of sight of the other men. His arms and thighs around her felt protective for a second. A raw surge of emotion hiccupped through her.

"Why do you want my photos? My journal? Does this have anything to do with my sister—do you know Dr. Jennie Flaherty? Do you know what happened to her?" Desperation pitched her voice high.

"I don't know anything."

"Then why did that man try to kill me? Why…"

…does someone named Sheik Bakkar Al Barrah want me dead?

But Kathleen clamped her mouth shut, instinct suddenly warning her to say no more. These men didn't know that she understood their Arabic dialect, that she'd heard them say a man called Bakkar had ordered the raid to kill her and her guards. This knowledge might serve as a tool to help her escape, and she needed to grasp at any advantage she could.

"That's better. Now stay quiet, don't struggle, and maybe— just maybe—we'll have a fighting chance at saving your life."

We.

He was pretending to be on her side.

But she'd heard him say she was his kill, and the only reason she was alive now was because he wanted to interrogate her first. She had to convince him he had the wrong woman. "If this is not about my sister, I think you've made a terrible mistake—"

"Yaaa!" He kicked his heels, and his horse took off in the direction her attacker had charged. She grabbed and hung on to the saddle horn for dear life. The other men mounted and with final, ululating, bloodcurdling shrieks of triumph, they thundered behind. The sky behind them glowed blood-orange as they charged into a sea of Sahara blackness.

Her savior had just turned abductor.

They journeyed for hours through the night, Kathleen fading in and out of consciousness, throbbing with pain, awakening from time to time to find herself cradled in Sayeed's strong arms, his rock-hard thighs holding her steady on the horse. Her mouth felt dry as dust, her throat thick. Nausea rolled through her stomach in waves. The entire Milky Way seemed to have shifted across the sky. Dawn was not far off. In moments of lucidity, Kathleen tried to replay the horror of the night's events in an effort to make sense of the overheard orders to kill her. And it dawned on Kathleen that Sayeed's English had been flawless and spoken with an American accent. For some misguided reason, that one, little, familiar thing in this hostile, foreign environment gave her a flare of hope, and she clung to it in her desperation. Because the other part of Kathleen understood the reality—injured, bleeding, barefoot, wearing only a ripped nightgown and with no food, water, map or mode of transport—she was entirely at this man's mercy.

Sayeed Ali was the one thing that stood between her and certain death at the hands of those other men.

But for how long would he keep her alive?

And if this was a weird case of mistaken identity—maybe they still wouldn't let her walk away after she'd witnessed them murdering her guards?

Fear, anxiety surged afresh through Kathleen, making her stomach churn. She concentrated on not throwing up, on staying lucid, but she grew dizzy again, once more fading into blessed unconsciousness.

The rocking motion of Sayeed's horse made Kathleen's buttocks move suggestively against his groin, her near-naked legs rubbing warmly against his inner thighs. He was a red-blooded male, and he had no control over what this physical massaging was doing to him. Not only that, the inherent vulnerability of his captive made him *want* to keep her safe, which fuelled his anger at her.

Kathleen Flaherty's mere presence in the Sahara had put Sayeed in a no-win situation and forced him to screw up big time.

He should have let Qasim kill her.

It would have cemented his cover with Bakkar.

But even though his CIA and FBI superiors would have deemed Kathleen Flaherty necessary collateral damage, Sayeed had not even been able to come close to allowing it.

Now, trying to keep Kathleen Flaherty alive could blow his alias and sink a multimillion-dollar, international, joint-agency operation. And that could cost the lives of thousands of Americans and other innocent civilians around the globe.

He swore to himself—he'd been sunk from the first instant he'd laid eyes on the woman. And that moment of initial indecision plus the subsequent chain of events had led to this—him taking his injured and vulnerable captive into the very dangerous heart of a Maghreb Moors' training compound. And the closer he brought Kathleen to Bakkar's lair, the more difficult it would be for them both to find a way out of this bloody mess alive.

Sayeed watched the dark forms of the other men as he rode. They flanked him, shadows in the night, but kept their distance. He could hear the chinks from harnesses, see the odd gleam of moonlight reflecting off metal.

Hyenas, he thought, waiting for first sign of weakness, deciding whom to back and where their own fortunes might lie.

Sayeed might have defeated Qasim in a leadership tussle, but the damage was done—he could feel his authority slipping.

He could also feel his captive slipping from life in his arms. She'd lost a lot of blood, and dehydration was a serious concern. He needed to stop soon, give her water, assess her injuries. Anxiety tightened in him. He dropped back a little from the rest of the posse. Once he was he out of earshot and immediate view of the other men, he unhooked his lambskin water pouch from his saddle.

"Kathleen?" he whispered, trying to offer her water. But although upright in his arms, she was totally unresponsive. "Stay with me, Kathleen," he murmured against her ear, the scent of her long hair, the feel of her skin against his cheek doing insane things to him. Deep things. Things that reminded Sayeed of who he really was—Rashid Al Barrah, an FBI agent under contract to the CIA, a man not used to the deep cover work he'd been doing for close to three years in this desert. He'd been forced to think of himself as Sayeed Ali, a dangerous man, a dark man, and in the process of living undercover in a terrorist camp, he'd begun to lose something of himself.

He'd been focused, numb, and that's just the way he wanted it.

Now she was stirring sensations, firing a protective instinct in him, and his alias was blurring. He resented her all the more for it. He reminded himself he was Sayeed. He had to stay Sayeed. Think of himself as Sayeed. Until this was over.

"Kathleen?" he whispered more urgently.

She remained silent, slumping from side to side as he rode. Urgency mounted in him. And as they came to a dry *wadi* bed, moonlight revealing a small grove of palms, he galloped up to the front of the posse.

"Halt!" he commanded, reining in his own horse. "We camp here for one hour."

The men came into a semicircle around him. Qasim reluctantly hung back at the periphery of the group, the tail of his black stallion flicking, the horse's coat gleaming with sweat in the moonlight.

"We should press on," argued Qasim. "Dawn is almost here"

"The horses need to rest," said Sayeed. "We stay."

"You're doing this for the girl. I say let her die."

"If she dies, we get no answers." Sayeed dismounted. He could feel them watching, waiting to see what he did with their injured captive. He took her down from the horse and carried her like a limp rag doll to the small grove of palm trees. The other men eventually moved a short distance away and made camp.

Returning to his horse, Sayeed removed the first aid kit he kept in his saddlebag. He carried it back to the palms, listening to the chatter coming from around the fire as the men boiled tea. Qasim's voice rose, strident above the others. "Sayeed talks nonsense—we should kill her now! Bakkar will see red if we arrive at camp with our target alive."

Sayeed took bandages out of the kit, along with disinfectant wipes and butterfly sutures. He rolled up a saddle cloth and gently rested Kathleen's head on it. But the movement caused her nightgown—split down the back from Qasim's sword—to slide off her shoulder and expose her breast. Sayeed stalled, bewitched by her sheer, female beauty. Her smooth, milky-white skin was haunting in the silver moonlight, the nipple dusky in contrast. He swallowed, quickly removing his turban and using the cloth to cover her. But his body had already reacted against his will again, and blood pulsed warm in his groin.

Sayeed was no different from the other men who lived at the compound. He had not seen the naked skin of a woman since he'd arrived at the Maghreb Moors' training camp over twenty-four months ago, nor had he been in contact with a woman for the nine months prior as he worked to infiltrate the cell and earn Sheik Bakkar Al Barrah's trust.

Gently, he moved hair matted with blood off her brow. "God knows why you came to this desert alone, Kathleen," he whispered, more to himself than her. "You are either very stupid or very damn brave."

She stirred slightly and moaned. Relief, tenderness washed through him. And he moved with more haste.

Thankful for the bit of moonlight, Sayeed tore open a disinfectant pad and began to clean away the blood around the gash on her brow. But his hand stilled as voices around the fire grew louder.

"Sayeed might be right," said one of the men. "That woman *had* to have told someone where she was going. And if she did, it's better we know who and when. We can then anticipate them or change plans."

"It's too late to change plans. The deadline is set, the airline tickets bought. The volunteers are preparing. Nothing can be altered now."

"Which is why we need to know if someone will come looking."

"If it's so goddamn important," countered Qasim, "let him interrogate her right here, right now! She could die on her way to the compound, and we'd be in exactly the same position as if we'd killed her back at the campsite."

"She's passed out. She can't talk now."

Qasim swore, lurched to his feet and flicked the last remnants of tea from his mug into the fire. Flames fizzled softly.

Sayeed had treated Qasim with kid gloves from day one. The man was violent, smart as a whip, an unpredictable and power-hungry sociopath. And although Sayeed had won Bakkar and Marwan's trust, Qasim remained leery of him.

But it was more than mistrust. Qasim had made it clear that his father, Marwan, should have given *him* more authority in the cell, not some outsider like Sayeed. And jealousy was making him dangerous.

Little did Qasim know Sayeed was in fact his cousin, the long-banished son of Bakkar Al Barrah. Bitterness filled Sayeed's mouth at the notion that he and Qasim shared common blood, that their temperaments perhaps resonated, that he himself could have become a Qasim had he not escaped his father's clutches all those years ago.

He opened the butterfly sutures and used them to carefully pull the edges of Kathleen's head wound together.

One man laughed suddenly, wicked, raw. "Ah, but Qasim, even if your Uncle Bakkar is angry, your *father* will be very pleased if we bring this woman to the camp, alive and kicking."

His was joined by even more raucous laughter. "Yes," said another, slapping his knee. "Marwan would bed a goat. This will be a grand prize for him—you will curry favor, Qasim, if you allow him to think it was your idea." The man snorted at his own joke. "Maybe he'll even put *you* in charge of our next raid."

The sound of a sword being drawn caused the men to fall silent

Sayeed tensed. He was suddenly conscious of where his own weapons lay.

An argument, yelling, broke out. Then came a grunt, a sick sound of a man dying. Followed by dead, heavy silence.

Sayeed's pulse quickened. He worked faster, knowing all the while the dead man was right, Marwan *would* become a problem when he saw Kathleen. Maybe he should have let her die under Qasim's sword—maybe death was better than possibly being brutally raped and sadistically tortured by the sadistic Marwan.

Memories of what had happened to his mother surged hotly into Sayeed's brain.

Crap.

Not only was Kathleen threatening his cover and the lives of thousands of innocent civilians around the world, she was making him vividly relive the most painful memories of his life.

She was reminding him of the real, underlying reason he'd accepted this mission—to kill Bakkar and Marwan, to regain his honor and his mother's by delivering justice, ancient-clan style. He planned to do it just after he initiated the special ops raid on the compound.

Was Kathleen going to cost him that, too?

Her eyes suddenly fluttered open. She gasped when she saw his face and tried to sit up.

"Easy," he said, restraining her by the shoulders. "If you get up too fast you'll faint. Here, you need water." He cupped the back of her head, gently lifting her so she could drink.

He wiped the water that spilled down her chin. Her gaze held his as she drank, and even in this light, he could read the confusion, the fear, in her eyes. She was seeing his face for the first time since he'd removed his head scarf to cover her. And Sayeed knew his features were not exactly avuncular—his aggressive bone structure, his dark eyes were more fearsome than friendly, especially in the silver monotones and shadows of the haunting moonlight.

"Who *are* you people?" her voice came out hoarse, a whisper.

"I told you, I am Sayeed Ali—"

"No, who are the other men, what do you all want with me?"

But before he could answer, a man began to approach over sand, the burden of bad news evident in his posture. He was coming to tell Sayeed one of their own had been murdered for slighting Sheik Marwan Al Barrah.

"Stay quiet, Kathleen," he whispered. "It's best they think you're unresponsive for a while yet. I've cleaned your wounds as well as I can for now. I'll look at them again later, at the camp."

"I don't want to go to the camp," she said.

"You have three options. Either you come with me to camp, or these men kill you, or the desert kills you. Take your pick."

Chapter 3

Dawn broke in a violent streak of orange, rippling color across the sand. The heat was instant, hitting Kathleen like a blast from a furnace. Thirst tightened her throat, and her brain felt thick.

Her captor had given her his turban and a scarf he'd found in his saddlebag. The turban cloth was now wrapped around her shoulders, covering the slash in her nightgown. He'd instructed her to drape the scarf over her head and cover most of her face as protection from sunburn. It was hot underneath the rough fabric, the wound on her temple throbbed and the cuts under her feet stung. Kathleen tried to ignore the discomfort by focusing on her surroundings. They were moving north, judging by where the sun had come up, and the terrain was gradually changing as they progressed—soft dunes rising in a series of steppes, the ground gradually turning hard and flinty.

Then, as if shimmering out of a mirage, the hazy outline of a cliff appeared in the distance.

Swaying in the saddle, trying to hold on, Kathleen wondered if it was real or a trick of the desert. Or if she was going delusional from blood loss, heat, shock, exhaustion. She allowed Sayeed's strong embrace to hold her steady. She had no other option. Without his support she'd lose her grip and fall.

The other men rode ahead, gaining distance. Kathleen realized Sayeed must have been intentionally dropping back because as the men crested a dune, momentarily dipping out of sight, he quickly reined in his horse, pulled the cork out of his water pouch and offered it to her. There wasn't much water left, and she drank deeply before he took the pouch from her hands.

"We must save what's left," he said, replacing the cork. "Just in case."

Kathleen noted he took no water himself. Without his turban, the sun burned fierce on his blue-black hair and his dusky skin gleamed. She couldn't help staring at him for a moment.

His features were assertive, aristocratic. He was beautiful in a harsh and smoldering way. His eyes were liquid obsidian, hooded, his brows arched high, his lips firmly sculpted, his skin smooth and the color of rich mocha. He was the stuff of Kathleen's desert fantasies—tall, dark, decidedly dangerous and utterly sensual—the kind of hero that populated her beloved tales of Arabian knights and desert conquests.

The effect was mesmerizing.

Disconcerting.

But more than anything, it was the naked directness of his gaze that met her curiosity in return. "You look surprised, Kathleen?"

"I…" She swallowed, thinking she must definitely be

delusional to be thinking her abductor was handsome. "Sayeed, please, just tell me what you want with me—why did you attack my camp?" *Why did Qasim say a man called Bakkar had ordered me dead when you didn't even know my name?*

He glanced away, at the horizon where the men had momentarily dipped out their sight line. His jaw tightened and his neck tensed.

"If this really has nothing to do with my sister, I think you've kidnapped the wrong person."

His eyes flickered, then narrowed sharply. "Cover your face properly," he ordered. "Your skin will burn. And you must stay covered at all times when we get to camp."

"I'm not going to camp," she snapped. "Not until you tell me why you kidnapped me."

He laughed bitterly, darkly in her face. "Go on, then," he said. "Jump down from the horse and run away. If those men over the ridge don't find and kill you first, the Sahara most certainly will. And believe me, I'll be happier to be rid of you."

She glared at him, resentment twisting into her fear. She was at his mercy. She *needed* him to survive and he knew it.

"If you'd be so happy, then why didn't you let them kill me back at the camp?"

"Bakkar, our leader, wants some questions answered first."

"Seems like the other men disagree with you." She paused, watching his eyes. "And you have an American accent. You learned English in the States, didn't you? Most people who learn English on this continent tend to learn it with a British accent. Or they speak French like in the Congo or German as in Namibia, Tanzania or Togo. Or Portuguese like in Mozambique or Angola, depending on what colonial power—"

"What in hell are you, some kind of encyclopedia?"

"I read a lot."

"Yeah, well, I travel a lot. That's how I picked up English."

"So you traveled to the States."

Irritability spiked with the rising heat in Sayeed. "It's none of your business."

"Who are those other men?"

"Criminals," he said quietly. "A band of desert thugs."

"Why do they want to kill me?"

"Because that's what they do, Kathleen, rob and kill people. And believe me, they could do a lot worse than simply kill you."

"Is that what you do, too, Sayeed Ali, kill people? Rob people, terrorize people?"

"Yes."

She stared at him, long and hard, her eyes like aquamarine pools, pure and clear, and in them Sayeed could read disbelief. For an insane moment, he was thankful. This woman didn't think he was all bad, and for some buried reason, he needed this right now. And *that* scared him.

He kicked the horse into action, and she grabbed wildly for the saddle horn to steady herself.

As they neared the shimmering cliff, the sun climbed higher and burned down hotter. Sweat pearled and trickled between Kathleen's breasts. She shaded her eyes, squinting at a strange formation becoming visible along the top of the cliff. "What are those ruins up there?"

"Just some old place," he said.

The plateau they were traversing began to funnel into a gully, the red stone cliff rising high on their right and another similar, crumbling wall of stone to their left. And as the valley narrowed, Kathleen felt a change in the body of her captor—a tighter tension in his thighs, a stiffness in the way he rode the horse. The gelding, too, appeared edgy, as if the animal knew it was nearing home—or danger.

Kathleen studied the men ahead. She thought she saw a shift in their postures, as well. The valley grew narrower, cutting off sunlight in places, rocky overhangs throwing sand into dark shadow.

Craning her neck, she squinted up at the ruins again. The structure looked like part of an ancient castle, constructed with red rock hewn from the cliff face itself. A small switchback trail lead precariously from the valley floor all the way to the top. "It looks like the remains of an old castle," she said. "Maybe even First Crusade."

He said nothing.

"See over there?" She pointed up. "You can tell by the positions of what look like the remains of turrets."

"How do you know about this stuff?"

"I…" She reminded herself to be careful about revealing too much knowledge or giving away the fact she spoke various Arabic dialects or that she lectured in ancient Arabic literature and knew the architecture of this region with the passion and love of a scholar. "I'm an historian. I've always had an interest in the history of this part of the world." She fell silent a long while, then spoke very quietly. "I just never thought I'd actually come here. At least not this way."

Sayeed felt bad. "Where are you from?" he said. He knew already, but it firmed his cover to ask these questions.

"Seattle."

"Pacific Northwest. Lots of rain."

She nodded, quickly averting her face, but he caught the gleam of tears in her eyes.

His heart twisted. And he felt his own pangs of homesickness. He missed cool rain. He missed the crisp fall days of D.C., the winter snowstorms, fireflies in summer. He'd been away too long. Living with his father and uncle had filled him with hatred for far too long. And this beautiful, young captive was grounding him, reminding him to hold true to his values.

The irony of the timing wasn't lost on Sayeed.

His values—the fact he couldn't allow her to become collateral damage—could cost the Pentagon and its allies this mission.

It could release a new, genetically altered, hemorrhagic fever upon the world.

In saving one woman, Sayeed could cost the lives of thousands.

What in God's name was he supposed to do with her now?

They rounded a bend in the valley, and the cliff walls suddenly squeezed in. Sayeed looked up, caught the glint of metal high along the rock face. He raised his hand in salute as he passed underneath.

A sentry high up in the rocks stepped out of hiding and returned the salute, his robes and turban ends snapping in wind that blew sharp and high along the cliff face. The sentry carried an assault weapon, and within arm's reach was a handheld rocket launcher. A similar sentry was positioned on the opposite cliff, strategically guarding the geographic gateway into to the Maghreb Moors' terrorist compound.

Sayeed could see Kathleen was noting their positions.

They now rode single file through the very narrow canyon, Qasim taking the lead.

Nerves skittered through Kathleen's stomach. She looked up again at the sentries and realized that if someone was to sneak right along the base of this narrow part of the cliff, the rocky overhangs might provide occasional cover from the direct sight line of the sentries. Already she was planning escape.

The gully suddenly ballooned into a wide, sun-drenched valley dotted with canvas military tents. Heavy weaponry, including what looked like missile launchers, were housed under camouflage netting, rendering them invisible from the air. In the distance, men were negotiating a rope obstacle course, someone barking commands.

"What is this place?" she whispered.

"Keep your mouth shut," Sayeed growled low under his breath. And she sensed real anxiety in him. This suddenly terrified Kathleen more than anything. It told her he was not in control here, and her life hung on how much authority he actually had in this camp.

The men dismounted. A handful of teenage boys swathed in dusty-colored robes came running toward them, averting their faces in submission. They took the horses, leading them into a corralled area that backed under a rock overhang which provided shelter for the animals. The men, however, lingered, waiting to see how Sayeed was going to handle their captive's arrival in the compound. Their eyes were hostile, some lascivious. Fear curled tight in her belly. Kathleen also averted her gaze, staring at the ground, praying they might release her even though she'd witnessed them murdering her Berber guards.

Suddenly, a quiet exchange seemed to ripple through the men. She heard the name Bakkar being whispered, and men began to step back. Sayeed got off his horse and reached up for Kathleen's hand. His gaze collided with hers, and the message in his face was sharp—*shut the hell up.* He yanked her down from the horse. She winced as her cut and swollen feet slammed to the ground.

Through the parting crowd came a tall, dark-skinned man dressed in a pristine white jalabiya cinched tightly at the waist with a colored and tasseled cord. Both a dagger and scimitar were also sheathed at his waist. A jagged and puckered scar twisted across his aggressive features from the left side of his brow down to the right side of his chin. It made his left eye droop sideways. In spite of herself, Kathleen stared, wondering if he might be blind in that eye.

The man came to a stop in front of her, but he didn't look at her. Instead he glared at Sayeed, waiting.

Her stomach turned to water.

"Sheik Bakkar Al Barrah," Sayeed said in Arabic, bowing his head deferentially. "I have something for you." He shoved Kathleen forward as he spoke. She stumbled into the circle, coming to a stop just a few feet from Bakkar. She shot Sayeed a terrified, backward glance.

His eyes were flat, his features implacable.

"Sayeed?" she whispered in terror.

"Get on your knees!" he demanded in English.

"Please, Sayeed—"

"Now!" Sayeed stepped forward, grabbed her shoulders, spun her to face Bakkar, and kneed her in the backs of her legs, forcing her to slump down into to the sand.

"Look at the ground!" he yelled.

Shaking, eyes burning, hurting, she did, her hair falling across her cheeks.

"This is the woman you wanted, Bakkar." Sayeed pointed at her, switching back to Old Arabic. Kathleen was certain now they had no idea she could understand.

Bakkar stepped forward, his hand going to the hilt of his scimitar, as if he might chop off her head right there. Slowly, he circled her. Kathleen watched his boots. She began to shake very badly. Her head wound began to bleed again. She focused on the dark spots of blood that dropped onto the sand.

"Why," said Bakkar, his voice very quiet, almost hoarse, "is she still alive?"

"We must interrogate her."

Bakkar stopped circling. "I gave you orders, Sayeed! Those orders were to kill that woman on sight!"

Sayeed's voice remained level. "She might know something that will be useful. She might have been relaying her position to a third party which could bring searches, international attention. We need to know exactly who she told what and be prepared. This captive *must* be interrogated. Otherwise it could cost—"

"*I* make the decisions!" Bakker snapped. "Not you." His feet turned as he faced the crowd of men. "Not anyone else here, but *me!*"

But one other man stepped out of the crowd, as if defying Bakkar.

Kathleen angled her head slightly so she could see the newcomer in her peripheral vision. He was tall—similar in build and stature to Bakkar—and he also carried authority in the set of his shoulders, the tilt of his chin.

"Or Marwan, of course," said Bakkar, noting him. "In my absence, my brother's word is as good as mine."

Marwan now walked slowly around Kathleen. She cast her eyes down, looking at his boots. They were polished to a gloss in spite of the dusty environment. He stopped directly in front of her, said in Arabic, "Tell her to look up at me."

Sayeed remained silent.

She kept her head down, praying Sayeed would intervene.

"Tell. Her. To. Look. At me." The low and menacing tone sent a chill crawling down her spine.

"Look up at the man," Sayeed said, quietly translating into English what Kathleen already understood.

She did. Slowly.

What she saw made her stomach slide. His eyes were like his voice—menacing. Black. With the unblinking stare of a snake. His features were a genetic echo of Bakkar's but uglier, even without the scar. His gaze was lascivious, his lips thick and wet, his hair pulled back sharply into a ponytail forming an angry widow's peak over a high brow. He smiled slyly at her, teeth devilish-white against dark skin. And Kathleen saw evil. She saw a dark heart. She felt it.

"Maybe—" Marwan said slowly. "Sayeed Ali has a point, Bakkar. This woman could be…rather useful. Once she's questioned, of course, and before she dies, naturally."

Silence simmered in the heat. Men shuffled.

Her chest heaved.

She heard a bird of prey calling up high above the cliff. And she knew she was doomed. She prayed that she'd simply have the strength, the courage, to deal with whatever was coming next.

"Fine," Bakkar said eventually. "Sayeed, you're the only one here who speaks English fluently. You do it. Get whatever answers you need, using any means possible. I don't care. Just bring me the information when you are done. Then you kill her." Bakkar shot a pointed glance at Marwan as he uttered the last words.

Marwan stared back, the smirk still curling his lips.

The challenge between these two leaders was clear. Bakkar was asserting his dominance by giving Sayeed control over their captive. And from the look on Marwan's face, from the way Qasim stepped slightly forward, Kathleen knew it wasn't going to be that simple.

"I want the information before midnight," Bakkar called over his shoulder as he strode toward his tent.

"It might take longer," yelled Sayeed.

Bakkar froze. Then he turned slowly, eyes burning, voice deadly low. "You have until midnight, Sayeed. Not one second later. Then kill her." He paused. "Or I will kill you."

Chapter 4

Panic clawed at Kathleen's insides—either she died, or they *both* died. She shot a terrified glance at Sayeed. But his face was hard, eyes like flint. And Kathleen was suddenly convinced that Sayeed Ali—a total stranger who'd already, strangely, stuck himself out on a limb for her—would not sacrifice his life, especially if she was going to lose hers either way. Why would he?

He grabbed her arm, yanked her up, began to drag her through the sand. Almost blind with terror, Kathleen stumbled and tripped behind him as she struggled in vain to get her feet under her. He reached a military-style tent, opened the flap and shoved her inside with such force that she slammed to the ground on hands and knees. He yelled terrible things at her in Arabic. Tears began to stream down her face.

Sayeed closed the flap that served as a door.

And was instantly silent. He stood stock-still. Fury crackled in his eyes, sweat glistened over his brow. He began to shake.

Kathleen didn't dare move. Humiliated, hurting, she stared at him, waiting for him to do or say something, but for several beats he seemed incapable of uttering a single word.

"Get up," he said finally. "Go sit on the bed."

Eyeing him warily Kathleen got to her feet and inched backward toward the camp cot. Gingerly she sat on the edge of the rough blanket covering the cot, her heart pounding so hard she feared she was going into cardiac arrest.

He stared at her for a few long minutes as if trying to decide what to do with her. "Wait there," he said. "I'm going to fetch my first aid kit, and if you step outside my quarters alone they *will* kill you. Understand?"

She swallowed, nodded, eyes filling with emotion.

He left the tent and Kathleen tried to inhale, pressing her trembling hands to her chest in an effort to calm her madly beating heart. She carefully surveyed her surroundings. She must be in Sayeed's private quarters, and they were sparse. A small fold-up table with a bowl and jug was positioned near the bed. A round shaving mirror hung over the bowl. There was a thin metal frame with a rod from which a few robes hung on steel hangers. At the opposite end of the tent was a narrow desk with a chair. A faded woven mat covered the floor, and a curtain had been tied back near the bed.

Hearing footfalls returning in sand outside the tent, Kathleen's heart began to pound all over again. The tent flap opened and Sayeed came in carrying a canteen of water, disinfectant, more bandages and a dun-colored bundle of clothes.

He set the pile of clothes on a chair, poured water into a tin mug, and offered it to her. But her hands shook so badly, she couldn't bring the mug to her mouth without sloshing water all over herself. Sayeed reached out and cupped both her hands around the mug with his own, steadying her enough to take several deep gulps. Up close, Kathleen could see a muscle throbbing at his temple. His neck was wire tense. So was his jaw. The scent of him was masculine, wonderful. And at this very moment he made her feel safe. She knew it was desperation making her feel this way—he was the only thing that stood between her and those killers outside.

Something softened momentarily in his liquid, black eyes as he watched her drink. But he quickly averted his gaze, set the mug on the table. And for a moment he stood still, his back to her.

"Sayeed?"

He turned, and Kathleen saw conflict in his eyes.

"What did that man say about me? Is he your leader?"

He inhaled deeply, dragged his hand over his hair. "Bakkar, yes, he's our leader. The other man is Marwan, Bakkar's brother and second in command."

"In command—as in a military camp?"

He ignored the question, instead pulling the small table up to the bed. On the table he set a bottle of disinfectant, bandages, cotton swabs and a towel.

"You're not going to tell me what Bakkar said?"

She needed to hear it from him, see if he would tell her.

"He just wants information, Kathleen. He wants to know why you are out in the desert alone—"

"I wasn't alone. I had two guides. Good men, and you killed them!"

"I didn't kill them."

"Your people did."

Anger tightened his features, but he said nothing as he poured water into a bowl. Kathleen reminded herself she was walking a fine line with Sayeed—she didn't know how far he could be pushed, and her life was in his hands.

"What else does Bakkar want to know from me?" she said quietly.

"Why you went to Adrar in the first place, and if you told anyone you were there."

She opened her mouth to speak, but he shook his head. "Not now. Let me do this first."

Kathleen fell silent, suspecting he was buying time for himself to figure out what to do with her. She'd heard Bakkar say he had until midnight.

Sayeed dipped a cloth into the water and began to wipe the blood and dirt from her face. His movements were so startlingly tender in contrast to his earlier actions that emotion balled painfully in Kathleen's chest. She struggled to hold it all in, but the sudden care in his touch was too much, and tears escaped down her cheeks.

Sayeed's hand stilled as he saw the tears. He swallowed, torment twisting his stomach into a knot. This was his fault. He should never have brought her here. He might have bought her a few more hours of life but then what?

He knew he couldn't kill her.

He also knew that if he didn't, he was toast. And so was the mission.

Sayeed *needed* to stay alive to press the button on the satellite GPS messenger he had hidden in his robes. Activating that button would send a one-way signal to the special ops troops amassing over the border. His signal would mobilize a military raid on the level-four lab hidden in the bowels of the castle ruins up on the ridge. And timing was critical. He could not press the button until all the suicide volunteers had arrived at the lab. And he had to press right after they'd been injected with the virus. The bombing of the castle would happen within exactly sixty minutes of his signal. The compound in the valley would be raided simultaneously, with a view to taking live prisoners.

Large, aquamarine eyes, glimmering with pools of emotion, lifted up and gazed at him. It was too much for Sayeed. He repressed an urge to wipe away her tears and distracted himself by properly cleaning the gash on her temple. She was going to have a scar, he thought. Then he almost laughed at himself—she wasn't going to live long enough for a scar. Damn, he had to do something to change that. He *had* to find a way to help this woman.

He poured disinfectant on a cotton pad and pressed it to the wound. Kathleen sharply sucked in air sharply, but said nothing.

He had to hand it to her. She might be a naïve fool to have come alone to this region of the Sahara, but she was brave. He could only admire that.

He applied more butterfly sutures, doing his best to bring the edges of the gash neatly together. Sayeed allowed his hand to linger briefly along the side of her face; he couldn't help it. Her skin was so smooth. "You got burned," he said softly. "You shouldn't have gotten so much sun."

She jerked away, her mouth tightening in anger. "And you shouldn't have attacked my camp."

"Glad to see you're feeling a bit better."

"Screw you."

He nodded. "How is the cut on your back?"

"Perfect, thank you."

Well, he sure as hell wasn't going to try touching her again—the woman had been through enough. "Fine," he said coolly, irritated with himself for showing he cared, for revealing he found her attractive. What in Hades was wrong with him?

Furious at the entire goddamn world right now, Sayeed pushed the pile of clothes into her hands. "Here's a robe and loose, cotton pants from one of the young stable hands. They should fit. There's water in the bowl over there to rinse your feet. And here are some shoes." He held out a pair of canvas slip-ons with rope soles. "Pull the curtain for privacy while you change." His voice was curt, and he knew it.

She glowered at him, then yanked shut the curtain dividing the rest of his quarters from the sleeping area.

Sayeed busied himself cleaning up the first aid stuff, desperate for a way to buy more time. They'd survived introducing her to Bakkar but only just.

And for now they were probably safe from Marwan.

But the clock was ticking.

He heard the sound of the curtain being pulled back, and he glanced up.

Kathleen had pulled her thick, red hair back into a ponytail, and it made her features look wan and fragile. The robes and pants fit well enough. The canvas shoes looked a bit big, but they were better than going barefoot.

Careful not to connect his fingers with hers, he handed her a bowl of dates scattered with a few nuts. "I'll bring more food later."

She sat on the chair, hungrily devouring his offering. Relief found its way into Sayeed as he noted pink returning to her cheeks.

"So," she said quietly around a mouthful. "Bakkar wants to know why I came to the Sahara?"

Sayeed nodded.

"You can tell him I'm looking for my sister, Dr. Jennie Flaherty. She's a molecular biologist who disappeared from a medical convention in Burkina Faso. She was invited there to be the keynote speaker on hemorrhagic fevers."

Sayeed knew this, of course, and so did Bakkar, but Sayeed said nothing, waiting for her to continue, hoping she'd let something slip that might be used to buy her life without getting him killed and—worse—blowing the operation.

"Jennie is a globally renowned expert on hemorrhagic

fevers. Ebola is…" Her voice lilted. The brightness of emotion and desperation filtered into her eyes. She paused, staring at the dates in the bowl as she struggled to gather herself. "Ebola is one of Jennie's specialties along with a recently discovered new strain, Ebola Botou. That's…that's why she was invited to Burkina Faso, to talk about it."

Sayeed knew this, too. It was why the Maghreb Moors had specifically targeted Dr. Jennie Flaherty, under direct order from their organization's mysterious leader, The Moor himself. Dr. Flaherty was one of the few people in this world with the potential to make the Ebola Botou virus airborne. And unlike the other Ebola strains, Botou had a unique incubation period and was genetically unstable. People infected with the strain would become contagious within fourteen hours yet show no outward signs until they suddenly succumbed about twenty-one days later. It was ideally suited for The Moor's biological suicide attack, especially if made airborne.

The Iranian scientist who'd started the work to make it airborne had committed suicide as he neared the end of his project eleven months ago, finding death preferable to what he was about to accomplish.

The Moor's plan had almost been scuttled, which was no doubt what the Iranian molecular biologist had hoped. Until the Maghreb underground, which kept tabs on such things, learned that one of the world's foremost experts who had the potential to finish the Iranian's work was coming to Africa, not far from the fringes of Sahara. Planning her abduction had been in the works two months before Dr. Jennie Flaherty ever set foot on African soil.

"I believe Jennie was kidnapped," said Kathleen.

"And why do you think this?"

"How else does one just vanish from right inside a conference hotel?"

"This is Africa. Stuff happens."

She leaned forward. "Yeah," she said, bitterness twisting her features. "Like being kidnapped from your tent and being held captive in a camp of desert thugs."

Frustration bit into Sayeed. This was not going anywhere useful at all. "Okay, so if you think your sister was abducted from a Burkina Faso hotel, what on earth brought you all the way to Adrar?"

"A postcard."

He raised a brow. "Your sister sent you a card from *Adrar?*"

"No, from Tessalit. Written in Gaelic, asking for help. I flew to Tessalit, started showing Jennie's photo around, and some villagers believed they'd seen her briefly in town, dressed in Berber garments. They thought she could have been traveling north with a group of men. Then a small group of Berber nomads came into town from the northeast, and one of the Berber elders said he'd seen a fair-skinned woman resembling Jennie crossing the Adrar Plateau with men on camels."

Bakkar would not like *this* information, thought Sayeed.

Dr. Flaherty had tried to escape in Tessalit. She'd managed to briefly elude her captors but was recaptured within hours—it must have been just long enough for her to dash off a postcard and perhaps give it to some villager to put in the mail. And she'd been smart enough to write in code, calling for help in a language no one could read, apart from Kathleen, apparently. The postmark would have revealed a location—a start point for a search.

"Why did you come alone, Kathleen?"

"Because," she said pointedly, quietly. "No one—not the U.S. State Department, FBI, Interpol, the Burkina Faso government or any other agency—was able to help me locate Jennie. And believe me, I badgered them all, for nine long months. It got so bad, I became convinced someone was hiding something, that I was being stonewalled."

Sayeed knew from his handler that Kathleen was indeed being stonewalled. U.S. authorities *had* been made aware—via Sayeed himself—that Dr. Flaherty had been captured by the Maghreb Moors and was working under duress in the level-four lab in the castle on the ridge. A decision had been made at executive level to leave her there until the raid. Any earlier move to extract Dr. Flaherty would have jeopardized the sensitive, joint, international operation. Unfortunately, at the behest of the Pentagon, White House, CIA, Kathleen Flaherty's sister had become a small pawn in a very big and dangerous game. It was unlikely she was going to get out alive.

"What else could I do but come here on my own? I'd already been to the newspapers, to political websites. I'd spoken with activists, met with my congressman, called the people at the university where Jennie worked. I set up a blog in her name, pleading for information. Nothing—not one thing—came from it all. How can someone just vanish, Sayeed? Into thin air? How come no one knows anything, yet people *saw* Jennie in Tessalit and on the Adrar Plateau?" She sat silent for a while, staring at the bowl in her lap as she worked to control her emotions. When she looked up, Sayeed's heart clutched. "I *had* to do this," she said quietly. "Jennie is… She raised me. She's the most important person in my life."

"What about your parents?" He spoke the question before thinking, and Sayeed realized something had just shifted in him. He was curious. He wanted to know more about her for himself. And he hated himself for feeling interest.

Her mouth flattened, and she glanced away.

"Kathleen," he said. "Please, talk to me. Anything you say might help me."

Her gaze jerked back to him. "Help *you?*" Distaste twisted her features.

"Yeah," he said curtly. "It might help *me* save *your* life."

"Why do you even want to?"

He stared at her for a moment. And he realized he wasn't really sure of the answer. "Look, I ask the questions here, and if you don't help, you're not going to live."

She lurched to her feet, bowl clattering to the floor. "I don't understand what's so important for them to get from me!"

"Sit down and just answer the bloody questions!"

She glowered at him, anger, frustration pinking her cheeks. "Fine." She seated herself slowly. "Have it your way. My parents were academics," she said, her voice going toneless. "My mother held a doctorate in philosophy and was so immersed in worldview analysis and her writing, she forgot she even had kids and a family. She left home when I was five. My father was an English professor who thought it necessary to bring a new fling home to his bed every few weeks. Other times, he'd stay out drunk for nights in a row. Jennie is twelve years older than me. She looked after me, made sure I bathed, had dinner. Got a bedtime story. Jennie—" Her voice caught. Tears gleamed in her eyes. "Jennie taught me everything. She…is my sense of home. My real family. I don't know if someone like you can understand that."

Someone like him.

Sayeed thought of his own family. His brutal father and uncle. His terribly scarred but beautiful mother. His own sense of loyalty to the now-deceased woman who had raised him and sacrificed so much to give him a decent life in the States. Sayeed's family was the reason he'd joined the FBI—to hunt bad guys like his father and uncle. To seek justice for people like his mother. It was the reason he'd taken this mission for the CIA.

It was the reason he was staring at Kathleen Flaherty right now, asking these questions.

And he felt for her because, more than anything in his life,

Sayeed had wanted a normal, wonderful family—a real sense of home.

"You're right," he said coolly. "A man like me doesn't get to have a real family. How can you be sure the card came from your sister?"

"I recognize her writing. And Jennie was the one who taught me Gaelic when we were kids—we used it as our secret language. The card also has a picture of an oasis on the front. Jennie used to say Gaelic was our oasis in a turbulent home, a language only we could understand."

"Any idea why someone would abduct your sister?"

Bakkar would want to know if Kathleen suspected anything or had told anyone of her suspicions.

"No. There's been no demand for ransom or anything. I know foreigners are kidnapped for money in some African countries. And people are abducted in places like Nigeria all the time by local groups protesting foreign oil interests and such. But Jennie wasn't involved in anything like that. Maybe it was a sex trafficking ring or some sort of human smuggling organization…." Her eyes filled again. She swallowed another ball of emotion.

Sayeed stared at her. This woman was so out of her depth, it was unbelievable.

"I can't decide," he said slowly. "Whether you are incredibly brave or terribly stupid to have come here on your own. The Sahara is not a place for a woman alone."

"Which is why Jennie needs me. I'm all she has left fighting for her right now. Jennie sacrificed so much of her youth for me. Now it's my turn. And if I don't make it out of this damn camp alive, at least I will have died trying to help her."

Damn, but in this instant, Sayeed felt a deep kinship for this woman. He got her. Wholly. Because he too would go to the ends of the earth for someone he loved, for family, for honor. In fact he had—it's why he was here.

"Does anyone back home know you were in Adrar, Kathleen?" he said softly

She sniffed, rubbed her nose. "No. The U.S. airline and travel agent I used know only that I went to Tessalit. I should have called and told someone I was following a lead to Adrar, but I'd become so numb from authorities not listening to me that I wanted to find concrete proof before I did." She paused. "If I did anything stupid, Sayeed, it wasn't in coming to the Sahara alone, it was in not making sure someone knew where I was every step of the way because no one is even going to know I am missing."

"You didn't even tell a friend?"

She cast her eyes down. "No."

Sayeed raked his hand over his hair. Bakkar would be pleased with this news. But then what? Once he told Bakkar, she was as good as dead.

She got up slowly from the chair, took a step toward him. Space in the tent shrunk.

But he didn't back away.

"But you know what?" she said very softly, taking another step closer to him.

He moistened his lips, his blood going warm at her proximity, his head buzzing with tension. "What?"

"I don't believe you. I don't believe a thing you've said—I think you know something about my sister. And that's why you took my box of photos from my tent."

Sayeed couldn't breathe. She was too close. He needed to think. He needed air. Needed to goddamn touch her. He backed quickly toward the tent flap before he did.

"Just…wait here."

Worry shot back into her features. "Why? Where are you going?"

Without answering, Sayeed stepped outside. He let the tent flap fall closed behind him, and he exhaled heavily. Dusk was turning to night, and the large fire circle at the center of the camp had been lit. Men were gathering around the flames, sitting cross-legged and passing round a hookah pipe as the younger boys set bowls of food and pots of mint tea on mats in the adjacent eating tent.

Sayeed climbed the boulders behind his quarters and sat for a while on the warm rock.

A gibbous moon was creeping above the castle ruins, throwing haunting stone patterns into relief along the ridge. And a downdraft had begun—cooler night air rushing down the cliff face to replace the residual day's warmth rising up from the valley. Sayeed watched the shadows around the fire, and he listened to the intermittent laughter. Bakkar and Marwan would be waiting for his report in a matter of hours. He rubbed his brow, tormented by the decision he was being forced to make.

Inside the tent Kathleen paced. She stopped in front of the metal rod where Sayeed had hung his robes. He'd looped his belt over the rail, and his scimitar was in the leather sheath. Adrenaline pumped through her. She reached out and fingered the handle. He must have his small dagger with him, but he'd left this larger weapon here. Could she use it? She swore to herself, then laughed somewhat hysterically. He hadn't left this by mistake, Sayeed *knew* she wouldn't hurt him. She was as good as dead without him to protect her. So how in God's name was she going to get out of this place? She spun around, paced some more.

She *had* to think positively.

She *had* to believe she was going to make it out of here—for Jennie's sake. If she died in this place, hope for Jennie died, too.

Sayeed was the key. Kathleen had to do whatever it took

to make him *want* to keep her alive. Which meant she'd need to bite her tongue.

She heard footfalls outside.

Kathleen jerked around as the tent flap opened. And froze in horror.

It wasn't Sayeed.

It was one of the other men.

He stepped slowly into the tent, his gaze pinning her, his features twisted in lust. He came toward her, slowly, menacingly.

Kathleen lunged for the scimitar on the rail, but it was too late. The man surged forward and flung the back of his hand across her face. Pain sparked and blackness spiraled through her brain. She bent over, bracing her hand on the small desk, trying to hold on to consciousness. The taste of blood filled her mouth. He came up behind her, clamped his hand over her mouth, forcing her to swallow blood. She tried to bite him, couldn't. He pulled her away from the desk, and in trying to hold on to the desk, Kathleen felt a pair of scissors on the surface that Sayeed had used to cut bandages. She clasped them in her fist as the man dragged her out of the tent and through the dirt.

Once behind the tent, he pulled her between some rocks and pushed her onto the ground. He pinned her flat on her back with his arm across her neck. Kathleen struggled to gasp in air as the man yanked up her robes and began pulling her pants down. Kathleen wriggled, tried to scream, but couldn't. Fabric tore. She suddenly realized she still had the scissors in her fist, and as the man tried to yank her pants over her buttocks, she stabbed him in the head.

He jerked back in shock.

Kathleen used the moment to scream and squirm out from under him. But as she tried to run, he dived for her legs, tackling her and slamming her back into the dirt.

Chapter 5

A terrifying scream cut through the night. Sayeed lurched up—*Kathleen! They were killing her!* He scrambled down the rocks, rushed to the front of his tent. The flap was open, no one inside. He heard her scream again. The sound came from somewhere in the rocks behind his tent. He raced round the back.

There, in the darkness, out of sight from the men around the fire, a close associate of Qasim's had Kathleen pinned by the neck to the ground and was lying on top of her.

Rage exploded through Sayeed's veins.

He drew his *jambiya* and lunged forward. The man rolled off Kathleen as Sayeed bore down, kicking up to his feet like an acrobat as he drew his own dagger. He flipped it into his hand and faced Sayeed, waving the blade back and forth as he rocked foot to foot.

Kathleen scrabbled backward through the dirt.

Sayeed kept his focus on the assailant. "Get into the tent," he growled at Kathleen as he and her attacker slowly circled each other, blades glinting. The man lunged. Sayeed dodged. Out of the corner of his eye, he could see Kathleen crawling on hands and knees toward the tent, pale skin showing through the rips in her robe. Adrenaline turned him violent. Sayeed thrust forward, almost slicing into his opponent's waist, but the man parried, circled, breathing hard, eyes glittering.

Sayeed circled, thrust again. This time he felt his blade connect with his opponent's flesh. The man swore violently and barreled forward. Before Sayeed could deflect the blade, the tip his opponent's curved dagger caught his hip, slicing a line of burning fire across it. Sayeed's heart pounded. He felt warm blood on his hip. He circled again, his body in a low crouch, muscles wire-tense, his blade held out front.

In the periphery of his mind, Sayeed was aware that the chatter around the campfire had gone silent. The men were all listening, but no one appeared to help or interfere. They were going to let Sayeed and the attacker sort this out themselves or fight to the death.

Out of the corner of his eye, he saw Kathleen returning around the side of his tent. Clutched in her hands was the scimitar he'd left inside the tent. Her assailant was momentarily caught off guard by her reappearance, and Sayeed used the moment to thrust forward. The man leaped backward, his heel connecting with a small rock. He tripped, falling hard onto his back. Air whooshed from his lungs. The impact seemed to wind and stun him for a nanosecond. Kathleen went for the gap, gripping the hilt of the scimitar in both hands, raising it high it over her head as she rushed forward.

"No!" Sayeed yelled. "Don't do it, Kathleen."

She hesitated, glanced at Sayeed.

"They'll kill you. There will be nothing I can do to stop them."

She seemed frozen in a moment of conflict.

"Put it down, Kathleen. Slide the sword over to me. Please."

Slowly, she stepped backward. She placed the weapon on the sand, kicked it over to Sayeed's feet. But as Sayeed bent to retrieve it, the man rolled onto his stomach and reached for his own sword that he'd left at the base of the rocks during his attack on Kathleen. Scimitar in hand, the attacker spun round and lurched back onto his feet. Screaming, he ran forward, blade raised high. Sayeed swung hard to his left as the scimitar came down. He blocked the man's sword with his own blade. Metal clanged against metal, the sound of connecting blades ricocheting up the canyon walls, echoing among the rocks of the castle ruins above.

Kathleen screamed and threw rocks at her assailant as she saw Sayeed take another strike on the hip. One of her rocks glanced hard off the man's forehead, momentarily stunning him. Sayeed went for the gap, his scimitar knocking the weapon from the man's hand and cutting through his wrist. Blood spurted. The man's eyes went huge in shock. He glanced in horror at his now useless hand as his blade clunked to the sand.

Sayeed rushed forward and hit him with his full body weight, tackling him to the ground. He then pinned the bastard to the dirt and pressed the tip of his scimitar to the man's throat. All he had to do was plunge it in. Sweat leaked into Sayeed's eyes, burned. He was breathing hard, bleeding himself.

But he could feel Kathleen watching, and he could not do it. He could not subject her to any more horror. He removed his sword, got up and kicked the man in the side. "Get out of my sight you piece of excrement!" yelled Sayeed. "Set foot near my quarters or my prisoner and I will string you up and gut you myself and leave you for the vultures. Understand?"

The man rolled away, staggered to his feet, clutching his gaping wrist. He stumbled into the darkness.

Sayeed turned his attention to Kathleen. In the moonlight she was sheet-white, her eyes dark with shock. Her face was dirt-streaked, and her robes were ripped across the chest, the swell of her breast showing underneath.

"Did... Did he..." Sayeed could barely speak, memories of Marwan raping and hurting his mother swirling fresh and red and violent through his brain, memories of Bakkar burning his mother's face with hot oil, blaming her instead of Marwan, scarring her beautiful face so no man would look at her again, banishing her from his compound, sending her alone and unequipped into the vast sands of the Sahara with her raw wounds. He began to shake.

"No," she said softly. "You got here before he could do anything." Emotion hiccuped through her, and she began to cry. "Thank you, Sayeed."

I am not Sayeed! He wanted to scream. *I am Rashid Al Barrah, and I will rip these men apart with my bare hands before I let them hurt you!*

Rage—raw like volcanic lava—boiled through his veins, his alias cracking around him. He grabbed her arm and, instead of comforting her, he hauled Kathleen around to the front of the tent and frog-marched her toward the silent crowd gathered around the campfire.

Faces looked up in shock as he shoved Kathleen in front of them. She stood there confused, shaking, her exposed skin alabaster in the moonlight.

Several men leaned forward. A few stood up, their hands going to the hilts of scimitars or daggers.

Others started coming out of tents.

Sayeed saw Bakkar open the tent flap to his private quarters and step out. Shadows from the fire played across his ugly scar—the scar given him by his eleven-year-old son. That boy was now a man, and Bakkar did not know it was the same man who held court in front of the fire now.

Marwan also came out of his tent.

Adrenaline thumped in Sayeed's chest.

"Now, you all listen to me." He pushed Kathleen forward and pointed his sword at her. "This woman, this prisoner, is *mine!*" He glanced at the face of each man gathered around the campfire. "And understand this—" he pointed the tip of his scimitar at the crowd "—if you or you or anyone one of you go near her, you *will* die. I have interrogated her. She knows nothing. Kathleen Flaherty is a stupid fool of an American who came to the desert looking for her sister when no authority would help find her. She is a laughingstock. And she has told no one she was going to Adrar."

He watched the eyes of the men, his gaze panning and settling on each and every one of them. "But she is good for other things."

Someone smiled, teeth glinting in the firelight. Sayeed pointed his blade at that man. "Yes," he said menacingly. "You know what I mean. I am publicly laying claim to this woman. I will take her for my wife, and the clan must accept this in the old way, the way that once made us strong. The way that some of you—" he pointed his sword at a close associate of Qasim's "—have forgotten. We need to remember where we came from. We need to adhere to our ancient codes of justice and honor." This time he looked directly at Bakkar. "*This* is why we fight. This, our past, our honor. And it's why we will be a force to be reckoned with once the world learns of our work. It's why organizations like Al Qaeda are already starting to look to us for manpower and assistance. This also means you will stay away from my wife or force me to invoke the code of justice and take your life or die trying."

Dead silence hung over the camp apart from the pop and crackle of the fire, the hiss of a boiling kettle.

Several men, including Qasim, glanced back toward Bakkar's tent. His silence was taken as tacit endorsement. Marwan, however, stepped forward, a sly smile forming on his face.

"You surprise me, Sayeed Ali," Marwan said quietly. "Perhaps even impress me. Take her, then. Let the old way rule." Marwan paused, his smile fading. "For now."

Sayeed seized Kathleen by the arm. He yanked her body hard up against his, and he pressed his mouth down on hers, forcibly kissing her in full view of the men while aggressively backing her all the way to his quarters. Claiming her, making her his.

Once inside his tent, he pulled back instantly, breathing hard.

Kathleen staggered, gripped the table for balance, her heart slamming hard against her rib cage. She stared in shock at Sayeed. Her lips burned from his kiss, from the rough taste of him inside her mouth, and her legs trembled in fear.

She understood exactly what he'd said to those men. She'd also felt the primal lust in his kiss, the hard press of his erection against her pelvis. Sayeed wanted her. And he had the power to take her right now, to do whatever he wanted with her, for himself. But he hadn't. He'd stopped.

He'd done this for her.

He'd put his own life on the line to save hers, again.

They stared at each other, the raw, strange, terrifying power of their kiss still resonating between them, swirling into the rush of adrenaline, of fear, of danger.

"Cover yourself!" he barked abruptly. Sayeed began to pace the room, his movements angry as if he was trying to distance himself, get away from her, get away from his own lust, but he couldn't because he was trapped in this tent with her, wild animals outside. He spun abruptly to face her. And

Kathleen saw that his body was shaking, his eyes glittering with emotion. "God, I am so sorry," he whispered.

She swallowed, unsure of what to say.

Sayeed steeped forward, cupped her face, his dark eyes liquid, gentle. "It was the only way. I…I told them I was taking you for myself, Kathleen, as my wife, and if anyone tried to touch you, I'd be bound by the ancient code of clan justice to kill them. And the kiss—it *had* to look like I meant it, Kathleen."

It sure felt like you meant it.

"What about Bakkar?" she whispered.

"I told him that you know nothing. I—" Sayeed swore again in Arabic. "I think he'll leave us alone for a while. I think they all will." He glanced down at her torn robes. "I'll find you more clothes," he said softly. "But not right now. I need to let things settle down outside. I need them to think we are… That—"

"That we're making love," she said quietly.

His eyes turned dark, hungry. "Yes."

Kathleen felt her cheeks warm. He averted his gaze, reaching instead for a cotton sheet. He handed it to her. "Can you use this to cover yourself in the meanwhile?"

She nodded, shakily wrapping it around herself.

"Are you *sure* that man didn't hurt you?" he said, his voice getting low and thick again.

"I'm sure."

He glowered at her, still pumped for a fight. Then he spun away and started marching up and down the room again like a caged lion.

Suddenly, he slumped onto a stool and put his face in his hands. He sat like that for a long while, face buried in his palms.

Kathleen drew the sheet tighter around her body, feeling awkward. She took a tentative step toward him. And without thinking she placed her hand softly on his broad shoulder. "It's okay, Sayeed."

Emotion surged through Sayeed. He didn't trust himself to look up or to say a word. This woman had been to hell and back—*he* had put her through that hell. He did not deserve her kindness, yet she gave it anyway. This woman was too good for him.

Too good to be in the godforsaken desert with these rabid thugs. Too damn good to be thrust into the heart of one of the biggest terrorist plots since 9/11.

"Sayeed?"

He lifted his head slowly. She knelt down in front of him, holding her sheet tight. Her face was grazed, dirty, her chin bruised. But her gaze was clear. "Why?" she said quietly. "Why did you do it? Why are you jeopardizing your life to save mine?"

He stared at her. Then he said, "Why do you jeopardize your own life, Kathleen, in an effort to find your sister?"

"I told you why," she whispered. "Jennie is everything to me. I love her. She raised me, and I owe her all that is good in my life." Kathleen paused. "I'm doing it because it's the right thing, Sayeed. Because I can't not do it."

"That's why," he said. "I helped you because it was the right thing. I couldn't not do it."

Just try telling that to the Pentagon when this mission goes to hell in a handbasket, when thousands of people start dying. All because he can't allow a woman called Kathleen to become collateral damage.

Sayeed swore softly to himself and felt like throwing up.

"I don't understand why you're with these men, Sayeed— you're different from them."

"It's not your business to understand."

"You just made it my business. You abducted and brought

me here. You put me in the middle of all this. I think that gives me a right to know."

She was right. He owed her an explanation, one he wasn't at liberty to give.

He got up, trapped, frustrated. Angry.

"Sayeed? Look at me," she demanded, her voice rising in frustration. "I'm not a fool. I can see this is some kind of military camp. You have heavy weaponry out there, missile launchers and things. It's all camouflaged from the air. I saw men doing military training exercises."

"That's what desert thugs do, Kathleen," he said curtly. "They deal in black-market weapons, raid tourist convoys—"

"And kidnap for ransom?" She looked him directly in the eyes, so directly he almost couldn't lie to her anymore. "Did your men take Jennie? Did something go wrong? Is that why there's been no ransom demand, because she's dead?"

His mouth went dry. "I told you," he said coolly. "I don't know anything about your sister."

"I don't believe it," she snapped. "I don't believe you came to my camp by accident. Your men have eyes in this desert, an information network. You must have, because clearly you have something very big here that you want to hide. And you took my box of photos, my journal but not my money. Why?"

"We took your money. We took anything of value."

"I don't believe you."

"Look, Kathleen. Your sister vanished in Burkina Faso. That's a completely other country. It has *nothing* to do with the men in this camp!"

"So why did you come to my camp?"

"To rob you. We heard there was an American showing photos around and traveling north. So we came to see if you had anything of value."

Her mouth went tight, and her eyes narrowed. "You lie. You came with orders to kill me."

A wariness stole into Sayeed. "What makes you say that?"

Her eyes flickered. "I… It's obvious. Isn't it?"

A slight chill crawled down Sayeed's spine. Had he underestimated this woman? Could she understand Arabic? Was she working him? "Kathleen," he said very quietly, calmly. "I know you've been through hell, but this is not about your sister, no matter how much you might want it to be."

Her shoulders sagged in defeat. The tip of her nose turned pink. "You really don't know anything about Jennie? Not one thing, nothing at all that could help me?"

"I'm sorry."

A single tear tracked down through the dirt on her cheek. "Can you promise me that's the truth?"

He almost laughed. "A *promise?* From *me*—the badass who abducted you? How could that possibly be worth anything to you?"

"You saved my life more than once. I've got a pretty good idea that you did it at huge risk to yourself. I trust you, Sayeed. I have to."

Trust.

His chest tightened. He fought the urge to comfort her, to tell her what he knew.

She stepped closer, her voice going soft, low. "Something tells me that, deep down, you are a good man, Sayeed, and that you really don't belong with these people."

His eyes burned. He ached with an unquantifiable need. To be touched, loved. To love back. He ached for home. He wanted her. He suddenly wanted all those things he'd written off, the things he couldn't have, and Sayeed knew that if he didn't step away from her this instant, he was going to make a very big mistake.

"There's water in the jug over there," he said curtly. "Clean yourself up. Take the bed, pull the curtain. You need sleep. I'll wait outside the tent until you're in bed."

Hurt flashed through her eyes, and she suddenly looked abandoned, defeated, small. Vulnerable. Alone. He could only imagine what she was going through right now.

Hell, if it might make her feel better, even just for tonight. If it kept her quiet. If it helped her sleep.

"I promise," he said. "I know nothing of your sister."

Sayeed stepped out the tent feeling he'd stooped to a new low, if that was even possible.

Chapter 6

Kathleen pretended to sleep, but through a gap in the curtain, she watched Sayeed bathe the wound on his hip by the light of a small kerosene lamp.

He stood naked, partially hidden by the small table on which he'd placed a bowl of water, and he was trying to see his wound in the small shaving mirror as he worked. The warm light of the lamp made his skin glow dark gold.

Dipping a cloth into the water, he wiped away blood. The gash didn't look too deep from Kathleen's vantage point, but the cotton pants he'd hung over the chair were covered in blood.

He opened a disinfectant pouch and winced as he touched the pad to his skin. Compassion surged through her. The wound was in an awkward position. She wanted to help but was embarrassed by how his nakedness warmed her cheeks, how it made blood pulse through her body.

He was beautiful, she had to admit. Powerful, sensuous,

dark, dangerous—just like every one of the desert knights and warrior sheiks she'd ever fantasized about. But that's all they were—fantasies—because although Kathleen liked to dream about swarthy princes on shining horses, men who could make her feel like a real woman, she didn't hold any naïve notions about the reality of men like that. Nor did she hold naïve notions about happily-ever-after marriages. She'd seen too many broken ones. Her own parents had been a mess. So had her childhood. Life, she knew, wasn't so simple.

And while she might have dreamed about being forcibly swept off her feet and whisked to a foreign and strange land, the truth of abduction was something else entirely. This naked man—this camp, this band of thieves—was no Arabian fairy tale. They were flat-out terrifying. And she was beginning to doubt she'd ever make it out alive.

Sayeed repositioned the small shaving mirror and moved around the side of the table for a better view of his gash.

Kathleen caught her breath as he stepped into full-frontal view.

His abs were classic washboard ripples. Black hair flared between powerful, smooth thighs. And he was big in a way that would satisfy the most demanding woman. Her nipples started to tingle, and her throat turned dry.

She tried to swallow.

She tried to focus on some other part of his body. Then she forgot herself completely, no longer pretending to sleep but watching with brazen fascination.

And as she studied his powerful physique, his smooth, even-toned skin, the way his dark, glossy hair gleamed in the lamplight and hung loose around his shoulders, the way his muscles rolled under his skin as he moved, her body warmed reflexively, and the memory of his fierce kiss returned. Heat pooled low in her stomach and a yearning began deep within

Kathleen—an awakening that had started with her journey to Africa and into the desert.

Then, as Sayeed struggled to affix a butterfly suture to his wound, he fully turned his back to her and she caught sight of a tattoo at the base of his spine. Shock rippled through Kathleen as she recognized the ancient Sun Clan emblem of a fierce Moorish tribe that once ruled a part of the Atlas Mountains.

Her pulse quickened. Only sheiks—princes—of pure lineage were permitted to carry that mark. She wondered if Sayeed had copied the emblem or if he could actually be a prince descended from the original Sun Clan.

She shook the notion.

What would a prince of the Sun Clan be doing with this band of marauders?

Sayeed must have sensed something in the intensity of her gaze because he suddenly turned and glanced at the curtain. Kathleen quickly closed her eyes, feigning sleep once again, feeling her cheeks heat with embarrassment.

Sayeed resumed his task, using the last butterfly bandage to close his wound. He pasted a length of clean, white bandage over the top, then, wrapping a towel around his waist, he sat topless at his small desk. He began to go through the pile of papers. Things grew quiet outside. Chatter around the fire ceased. So did the noises of pots being cleaned. The desert shifted its cycle as night creatures came out to rustle and hunt. Kathleen heard a distant yipping, possibly jackals hunting high on the cliff. She pulled her sheet tighter around her, wishing she had some pajamas. But sheer exhaustion finally overcame her, and Kathleen fell into an unsettled slumber.

Sayeed drew back the curtain gently, making sure his captive was still asleep. His chest tightened as he gazed down at her—she was even more beautiful in repose, if that was possible. Hair like flame spread over his pillow. Her lips, full, were slightly parted as she breathed. Her chest rose and fell gently. Again, he recalled the shape of her breast, the smooth, alabaster skin. He felt himself harden again, and this time he allowed himself to savor the sensation of arousal between his thighs, watching her a few seconds longer, just imagining what she might feel like under him. She murmured, turned.

His pulse kicked. He quickly pulled the curtain back into place, then returned to his desk. He seated himself and picked up the pile of photographs his men had taken from Kathleen's tent.

They were mostly pictures of Dr. Jennie Flaherty—the ones Kathleen had been showing around to villagers. And the responses to the pictures had led her north into the Sahara, in the direction of their camp. Which is what had brought her to Bakkar's attention.

From that moment, she'd been doomed.

Flipping through the pile, Sayeed came to a photo of Kathleen and Jennie together in a cabin of some sort. It looked like Christmastime, a wreath on the door, snow piled high against frosted windows. The two sisters were pink cheeked and smiling as they cradled red mugs of steaming cocoa with tiny marshmallows floating on top. Sayeed studied Kathleen, thinking she was everything he'd ever lusted after in a woman. She had a glow of health, of pure living. Her curves were all woman, and she radiated sensuality. He loved her pale skin, her thick, red hair, her clear, aquamarine eyes—a man could drown in those eyes.

They appeared to twinkle with some secret as she looked toward the camera, and Sayeed found himself wondering who had taken the photo—a boyfriend, perhaps?

He wondered if she had a man in her life. He thought not—Kathleen had told him Jennie was the most important person in her life. A significant other would be here in the desert helping her if he was worth his salt. And Sayeed had noted Kathleen wore no rings on her fingers. He guessed she was very much single. A ripple of excitement, of possibility, reached his consciousness before he shunted it out of his mind. What a ridiculous thought. Where in hell had that come from anyway?

Even if they did make it out of the Sahara alive, even if he did look her up in the States once this was all over, Sayeed wouldn't stand a chance. Not only had he brutally kidnapped and manhandled her, he'd lied to her about her sister, the most important thing in Kathleen's life. He had a good sense she wasn't going to get over that lightly.

Kathleen Flaherty was the kind of woman who put a lot of stock in a promise.

He returned his attention to the Christmas photograph of Kathleen and Jennie, again noting the genetic similarities and differences in the siblings: the taller, more angular and much older Jennie and her pretty little sister, twelve years her junior. A new and deeper respect for Dr. Flaherty filled Sayeed. It couldn't be easy to give up one's youth to raise a kid sister. Damn, these two, he liked them.

He thought of Jennie Flaherty locked in the level-four lab, being forced against her will to make the Ebola Botou airborne, working almost 24/7 to meet the deadline set by The Moor, the mysterious leader of the organization known simply as the Maghreb Moors. It must be killing Dr. Flaherty to know what they were going to do with her work and to think of her sister worrying about her.

He flipped to the last photo. It was an old one—Kathleen, maybe six years old. Which would make Jennie about eighteen in this photograph. Kathleen had mentioned their mother left home when she was five, so this picture could have been taken about a year after their mother abandoned ship. Jennie's arm was tight around little Kathleen's shoulder. They looked sad.

Inhaling deeply, Sayeed turned his attention to the diary.

The old leather and thick pages gave it a nice heft, but it was not the ideal journal for traveling, especially in a digital world. He thought of her fountain pen, her old-style cotton nightdress, how she knew about the crusades. Kathleen had a respect for the past, for things that took time and hard work. Those were the things she sought to preserve.

She rolled over in her sleep, murmuring. Sayeed tensed, expecting her to wake. He wondered what she was dreaming. A nightmare perhaps. She'd seen her guards killed. She'd been kidnapped and assaulted. Her head must be filled with horrible images. Guilt twisted through him.

He opened the cover of her journal, turned the pages and began to read.

Slowly, increasingly, Sayeed became overwhelmed by her beautiful, lyrical prose, her descriptions of this desert he'd been born in and banished from by his own father.

But while he'd returned to the Sahara with vengeance in his heart and a death mission on his mind, she'd arrived with wide-eyed wonder and compassion. And she was painting with her words images he'd forgotten over the years and been blind to upon his return.

He was seeing it all anew through her eyes—the colors and the scents of the desert, the sounds of his people—and Sayeed felt his kinship with Kathleen deepening inside him.

She was reminding him what was true. And what was worth fighting for.

Sayeed read into the night while she slept.

Her journal affirmed that Kathleen was a fierce defender of those she loved. Loyal. A loner. A romantic at heart with a yearning for a sense of real family she believed she'd never have. Even in her innocence, part of her was jaded, thought Sayeed, and suddenly he wanted to show her—and himself—it *was* possible. And that shocked him.

He shook himself.

He was fatigued. His muscles burned, and his wound throbbed. He needed to find a few hours' sleep himself.

His quarters were small. He could lie on the floor, canvas over hard-packed sand, which was a bitch to sleep on. Or he could lie on the edge of his camp bed beside Kathleen. He argued with himself the floor was the wiser option.

But a secret part of Sayeed—the part that was still Rashid, the part she was reawakening—wanted, *needed* to be close to her, to smell her hair, her skin, to feel her soft warmth. It was a deep, human need to connect with the person he was coming to know through the pages of that journal and through their forced proximity. And Sayeed argued that if he slept close to her, he had a better chance of protecting her through the night from those barbarians outside.

He pulled on a light pair of white, cotton pants, turned down the lamp so there would still be some light if she woke afraid in the night. Then, carefully, he edged onto the cot. It creaked under his weight, and he stilled. But she didn't stir. She was curled over in the far corner against the canvas wall. He lay gingerly on his back, right on the edge, just listening to her breathe, thinking it had been a long, long time since he'd spent a whole night with a woman.

It made a change from his past relationships.

Sayeed had never dated a woman he wasn't sure he could walk away from. He wasn't even really sure why. Perhaps it was his lifelong obsession with killing his father and uncle, as the ancient code of Sun Clan justice decreed he must, that stopped him short of seeking commitment.

Or maybe it was because he hated something deep within himself—he carried the genes of his father and of Marwan. And Qasim. How much like them was he really? Did he even deserve a woman like Kathleen or a shot at a proper family life?

And once he killed them? Could he ever go back to the FBI, to who he'd become in America? Or would he be throwing away everything his mother had sacrificed for him?

Was there a time to cut the past adrift and focus on the future? Could he even do that?

Kathleen rolled over onto her side next to him, murmuring again. The sheet she'd wrapped around herself slid off her torso, and Sayeed felt the soft, rounded warmth of her breast against the bare skin of his arm. He focused on keeping dead still as he stared up at the tent roof listening to the sound of a beetle bumping against the canvas, seeking a way in. But then he felt her hand touching his chest.

His pulse quickened. His mouth turned dry.

She murmured again in her dream and cuddled closer to him, seeking comfort. He could feel more of her body, her bare skin. She was smooth like silk, warm. Soft.

Her hand moved slowly down his stomach, and her leg hooked over his. Sayeed didn't dare take a breath.

She was dreaming, wanting him in her sleep.

His body went hot. His heart began to race. His erection grew hard, urgent, his blood throbbing loud against his eardrums.

He turned his head to the side. Her face was right there, eyes closed and lids fluttering. Her lips were deliciously parted. He breathed in slowly, just inhaling her breath, her scent. Her mouth was so close. Unable to stop himself, he touched his fingertips gently, illicitly, to her lips.

Her eyes flared open in shock. He pulled his hand away.

She stared at him, her pupils darkening.

Chapter 7

Kathleen was mortified to find herself half-naked in Sayeed's arms, her leg over his thigh. For a paralyzing moment she thought she might still be dreaming that she was making love with a dark and dangerous Moor, a fierce, desert prince with the mark of the Sun Clan.

But when Sayeed tried to move away, and she felt his skin hot against the inside of her thigh, fire shot to her belly, and she realized she was most definitely awake. Lust sparked with adrenaline through her blood, making her heart beat faster, blurring her mind. And before she could even think, before he could extricate himself from her slumberous embrace, Kathleen touched her fingertips to his lips, feathering the sculpted outline of his mouth. His eyes turned dark, and his breathing changed. She could feel his muscles quivering with the tension of restraint, and her heart began to race so fast she felt dizzy.

Kathleen closed her eyes and pressed her lips against

his. She tried to tell herself this was foolish. This man had abducted her, and she knew nothing about him. She might never make it out of the Sahara alive. But maybe that's what drove her now—a need to affirm life, to *feel,* to make love before she died.

Sayeed drew her tentatively into his arms, as if in question, allowing her plenty of opportunity to pull away, and when she didn't, he kissed her back, his tongue exploring the sensitive, inner seam of her lips. Kathleen's mind swooped with pleasure. Heat rushed to her belly. She murmured, kissing him as she hooked her leg higher over his, and she felt her nipples hardening against the bare skin of his arm.

Sayeed thrust his fingers into the hair at the back of her neck and drew her closer, his kiss becoming more aggressive, more urgent. Her mind spiraled as his tongue went deeper, tangling with hers. And suddenly Kathleen didn't care that she was a captive somewhere in the Sahara, being held in an enemy camp. She *couldn't* think about anything other than savoring the sensation of this very moment.

"Kathleen," he whispered, pulling back slightly, his voice thick, his lids low, eyes dark with desire. "We shouldn't, not after—"

But she drew his head back down, kissing him hard, demanding. Angry. Afraid. Craving the raw, physical release of the emotional energy trapped inside her, not wanting to think about how close she had come to losing her life. Or what might happen next. She kissed him fiercely, as if there might be no tomorrow, and she was going to take every little bit out of today.

He seemed to sense this, because again he pulled away, and this time he held her face firmly between his hands, his gaze penetrating, smoky, hungry, almost dangerous. Her blood pounded.

"Kathleen, are you sure?"

Her answer was to reach under the covers and trail her fingertips over the muscled ridges of his abdomen, her hand inching lower and lower toward his groin.

She felt his sharp intake of breath as her fingers touched the hair low on his belly, and inside she smiled. He yanked her hard against his body, and she felt his large, rough hand stroking up the outside of her thigh, over her hip, along her waist, until he cupped her breast, the rough pad of his thumb rasping over her sensitive nipple. Heat condensed into liquid-like fire between her legs, and Kathleen felt drunk, delirious. Her fantasies—all the romantic desert stories she'd ever read—came swirling to life in her mind, mixing and melding reality with dream. She could not believe she was actually in bed with a dark and dangerous Moor, and hell, she could fantasize he really was a Sun Clan prince in disguise if she wanted and that he was just living temporarily with a dark band of Ali Baba thieves. His hand went to her belly, then lower, and she gasped. He was melting her from inside out, and she became filled with a desperate urge to open to him, to feel him touch her between her legs. Kathleen angled her thigh higher over his body, giving him access. And she began to shake in anticipation as he teased the inside of her thigh with his fingertips, getting closer and closer.

Then suddenly, he cupped her, and she groaned in sensual pleasure as he sunk his finger inside.

She moved against him, her need growing desperate and fierce.

Sayeed sank another finger into her, and Kathleen's breath hitched slightly on a small, distant spark of fear, but she was ready for him, had never felt more ready for this. She moved her pelvis, heightening the sensation, desperate, aching desire driving her.

He suddenly flipped her onto her back, knelt over her and stared down at her nakedness. Approval was written into his handsome, dark features, and the desire in his eyes was raw. He'd left the kerosene lamp on low, and the bare skin on his chest gleamed in dark contrast to the white, cotton pants gathered and slung low at his waist. His black hair hung glossy and loose about his impressive shoulders, and he was breathing heavily. He asked her again. "Kathleen—"

She shook her head, shutting him up as she reached out and began rolling the loose, cotton pants down his hips.

A twinge of apprehension braided into her desire as she saw the dark flare of hair between his legs and the size of his arousal. She swallowed, but continued rolling his pants down farther, revealing the white bandage over his hip—a wound he'd received saving her. Reality crawled back into the edges of her passion. So did a moment of doubt. She touched the bandage.

He didn't wince, didn't flinch. His black gaze held hers, pinning her to the pillow, devouring her, his chest rising and falling. He placed his hands between her knees, and, slowly, he opened her legs wide.

Kathleen swallowed another spurt of anxiety as he lowered himself over her and entered between her legs with just the tip of his erection. Hot. She almost fainted as her mind rushed and spun like a fairground ride.

Slowly he pushed deeper, the quivering in his arms showing how much his restraint was torturing him. He moaned in pleasure as he sank a little deeper inside her, teasing her ear with his tongue, his breath sending warm, drugging waves through her entire body.

He pulled himself out a little and thrust back harder, a little less controlled. He did it again, this time thrusting all the way to the hilt, with a groan of lust. Kathleen arched sharply under him and gasped as a sharp, tearing pain radiated through her body.

He froze in shock.

His gaze shot to hers.

And the question was sharp in his eyes. He started to withdraw.

"No, please," she whispered, arching up to him, holding him in.

"You're a virgin?" he whispered.

Tears of pleasure rolled down her cheeks, and she nodded.

Again he tried to extricate himself. But she shook her head. "Please, Sayeed, I want this. It's beautiful."

He entered her again, very slowly this time, gradually filling her with his warmth, allowing her to accommodate him. The skin all over her body turned sensitive, every nerve ending awakening, tingling, her cheeks growing hot as pleasure radiated through her core.

He began to take her faster, faster, and she grew wetter, warmer, hotter until she felt a scream rising from somewhere deep in her chest. She could feel his whole body begin to shake, and she could feel an almost electrical quivering inside her. Then, as he plunged deep into her, he froze and shuddered with release, holding her close, murmuring Arabic words into her hair that she could not catch.

Sayeed was overwhelmed to learn he'd just taken a virgin. He felt truly bound to her, truly responsible in ways he couldn't begin to describe. He *had* to protect this woman now. And as he held her in his arms, he vowed he would. No matter the cost. And he could feel this new goal suddenly beginning to assume equal, if not greater, proportion to his sense of duty to his adopted country and to this mission.

Sayeed looked down into her eyes—large pools still filled with the darkness of desire.

"Come on top of me, Kathleen," he whispered in English.

She seemed suddenly embarrassed, as if she'd failed in

some way. He stroked the side of her cheek. "You'll feel more that way."

He swung her on top so that she straddled him. And the sight of her totally naked on top of him stole his breath. Red hair glowing like fire in the yellow light of the kerosene lamp cascaded in waves over her pale breasts. Her nipples were still tight and pointed with desire, her skin glowing with a sheen of perspiration.

Sayeed grasped her hips. "Move like this," he whispered, watching her face as he began to rock her back and forth on top of him. She let him direct her movements, and then he saw the change in her face. She began to move on her own, fuelled by her own desperation, riding him hard, her hands braced on his shoulders, her skin rubbing against his as she opened her legs wider, sinking lower onto him, making him go deeper. She moved faster, hard rhythmic strokes increasing in tempo until she was almost panting, and suddenly she arched her back, her nails digging into his skin as she thrust her head back and came with a sharp cry.

She sank down on top of him, warm, soft, relaxed, and Sayeed just held her in silence, stroking her hair, feeling himself go soft inside her.

"Why didn't you tell me this was your first time, Kathleen?" he said eventually.

For a long while, she didn't reply. It was as if she was choosing not to make it real by talking about it, as if she didn't want to invite back harsh reality. Or think about where they might go from here.

"I don't know," she whispered finally. And surprisingly the response hurt Sayeed. Something deep down wanted it to be about him. But how could it be? She didn't even know who he was.

She looked up at him and smiled, but her eyes were sad. "I...think I dreamt about you before."

"I don't understand."

"I mean, this is as true as my dream will ever come. I... just needed to grab on to it. Don't ask me why."

"What dream?" Deeply curious now, Sayeed thought about the words in her diary—Kathleen had confessed to dreaming about the desert, but she'd also written she'd never have had the courage to come and walk these sands, ironically, had Jennie not disappeared here.

She pulled the sheet higher over her chest, a little self-conscious now. "It doesn't matter what dream."

It did matter, more than Sayeed understood why.

He realized, also, how much he'd slipped out of his undercover persona, how much power his captive—this compassionate, beautiful woman—held over him. Not once while making love had Sayeed thought about his cover identity. And the man who lay holding Kathleen in his arms right now was him, Rashid Al Barrah, banished prince of the Maghreb. Somehow this woman had reached inside him and touched the truth, and she didn't even know it.

He moved a strand of hair back from her face. "How old are you, Kathleen?"

He knew she was twenty-five. He'd seen that from her journal.

Her features tightened. She wrapped the sheet more tightly around her body and got out of bed. She went to the table and poured water from the jug into a mug. Her hair was a disheveled mess, her cheeks glowing. She looked so damn sexy Sayeed wanted to take her all over again. But something inside her had switched. And Sayeed could see their magical moment was over, gone.

"Kathleen?"

She turned to face him. "It's irrelevant, Sayeed."

"It's not irr—"

"It is! You're just asking because you can't figure out why I've never slept with a guy."

He got out of bed, came over to her, raised his hand to touch her. But she backed off and his hand fell limp to his side. "It's just that you are so beautiful, Kathleen. So desirable. You're brave, compassionate, intelligent. You've shown you will do anything for those you love—you're everything a man could want."

She laughed, softly, a little derisively. "What kind of man? Not the kind I'm looking for. Not the kind I've ever dated. What I thought I wanted doesn't exist, Sayeed."

"What do you mean?"

"I'm old-fashioned—there, I said it. I'm an idealist, a romantic. I wanted a guy who'd stick around for the long haul, not a one-night stand. I wanted someone with the same values as mine, someone I could build a life, a family, a home with. That's why I waited. Guess I gave up." Her voice held a tone of resignation, and her eyes were empty. She drank her water.

He watched her, wishing he'd made her happy, that sex had been better for her. That he hadn't been a compromise. That he wasn't a one-night stand.

"The sex, it wasn't what you expected, was it?"

She looked at him in surprise. "God, no. I—" She blushed. "It was everything." She hesitated. "And more"

"Then tell me why you gave up."

"You'll laugh." There was no mirth in her eyes.

"Try me, Kathleen," he said.

She moistened her lips and inhaled deeply, as if debating whether to spill. Then she shrugged. "I'm probably never going to get out of this camp alive, Sayeed. Maybe I just wanted to make love before I died."

He laughed dryly. "You've just managed to make me feel used, Kathleen." He reached for a towel, wrapping it around his waist. "Guess I had it coming, being this end of a one-night stand for a change."

"You see, I rest my case. Most guys—especially ones that look like you—don't commit to a woman like me when they can bed anyone they choose, anytime they like. Why would they?"

"You don't know anything about me, Kathleen."

This time she laughed.

Sayeed swore to himself. He was digging a hole here, opening himself up, but something had changed in him. Not only did he want to keep this woman safe, he felt a need to tell her who he was, to come clean about why he was here. He wanted to share his secret with the woman he'd shared his body with.

And he was beginning to think she was exactly the kind of woman he might want to spend his life with, make a family with, build a home with. A real one.

And it struck him that if he followed through and killed Bakkar and Marwan, he might not be able to do that.

Not only had Kathleen assumed equal importance to his mission, she was making Sayeed question the very goal that had driven him back to this desert—his duty as a Sun Clan prince to avenge a heinous crime. Sayeed suddenly felt as if he'd come to a strange crossroads, and oddly, he felt lost.

"What makes you think you won't find a man with the same values as you, Kathleen?"

She finished her water, set the mug down. And he could see pain in her eyes. "Maybe they think they have the same values, Sayeed. Maybe at some point both partners actually do think they want the whole monogamous, long-term commitment thing, to build a family and grow old together. Then comes the crap life throws at you—and the bickering starts, and the affairs…." Her voice faded.

"Your parents really hurt you."

"They should never have been parents." Bitterness laced her words. In her eyes, there was a sudden hardness.

And he felt even more responsible. Sayeed suddenly wanted to show Kathleen that her dream *was* possible. He wanted to show her he had the same values. And it shocked him. Because it was true—he really did want a real family, a home. One woman in his life, someone he could grow old with.

He'd buried it away and she'd forced it out of him, changing him in some fundamental way by just being Kathleen. And now it was all going to clash head-on with his mission because the powers that be would still see her and her sister as necessary collateral damage. While he, on the other hand, selfishly wanted to keep her safe for the future. For himself.

But before he could think another thought, a curt command sounded outside the tent. Kathleen's gaze shot to the door, fear in her eyes.

Sayeed hurriedly grabbed some clothes.

"Get dressed," he said curtly. "Take one of my robes."

Kathleen pulled on one of Sayeed's large robes, tying it at the waist with cord as she listened to the urgent whispers in Arabic right outside the tent wall. Sayeed was talking to another man whose voice she hadn't heard before.

"The volunteers are all at the castle," the man said. "It's going down at 1900 hours tonight. Bakkar wants you up at the lab when it does."

"Why?" whispered Sayeed.

"Because he wants you to kill Dr. Flaherty when she's done injecting the volunteers."

Kathleen's mouth went bone dry. Chills, sweat prickled over her body.

He knew!

Sayeed knew exactly where Jennie was.

Hands shaking, she leaned closer to the canvas, not wanting to miss a single word.

"Why must *I* do it?" Sayeed hissed. "I was going to stay down here, leave with Bakkar and his men."

"Bakkar let you keep the sister. He said this is how you will repay him. I suspect this is his way of ensuring your loyalty, and he wants you to do it in the lab as soon as she's completed the last injection."

Rage pounded into Kathleen. But she didn't dare move lest they hear her.

"No," said Sayeed. He sounded angry. "Dr. Flaherty must live until we are sure the plan is working. If we kill her too soon, we won't know for sure if the Ebola Botou is truly airborne, and we'll have no one to help us do another batch. Let her inject the volunteers, then I will take her into the desert while the volunteers travel to their destinations. When innocent civilians start dying around the world, when people realize we've just unleashed the biggest biological suicide attack on the western world to date—*then* I will take her life."

Kathleen's heart turned to cold stone. Never in her life had she hated a man more than she detested Sayeed Ali right now. And beyond hatred she felt stupid, used.

There was silence outside the tent. A cough. Then the man said. "Come, you must tell Bakkar this yourself."

Footsteps crunched in sand, then grew faint.

Kathleen slid slowly to the ground, held her knees. Mortified. *Sayeed was a terrorist.* He'd lied about Jennie. She was captive in that castle, and she was going to die.

Kathleen began to shake. They must have abducted Jennie from the hotel in Burkina Faso because she had the skill to turn the Ebola Botou virus into a biological, human time bomb. Jennie had once told Kathleen how frightening it would be if something like Ebola Botou became airborne, and she'd said it could be done. That's why these bastards must have specifically targeted her.

And *that's* why Bakkar had ordered his men to come to Kathleen's camp and kill her, in case she'd led people to uncover this plot.

Blood drained from her head. She'd slept with the man who was going to kill her sister along with thousands of innocent civilians around the world.

Kathleen launched to her feet, panic slicing through her, sweat breaking out over her body. She had to help Jennie. And she had to warn someone about the imminent biological attack.

But she didn't have much time—she'd heard the man say it was going to go down tonight at 1900 hours.… Oh, she could not believe this was happening.

Focus, Kathleen. Think. You've got to leave before Sayeed comes back. Take what you need from his tent and go….

She found the pair of shoes he'd given her earlier, and she pulled on a pair of his cotton pants, rolling the waistband over several times to make the legs shorter. She tightened the large robe over the top and quickly wrapped her head in a piece of turban cloth, leaving only her eyes showing through a slit. She'd need water out in the desert. Kathleen glanced at the jug on the table, wondering how she could carry some, but stilled as she heard footsteps crunching in sand outside.

She spun round.

The tent flap opened.

Kathleen froze like a deer in headlights.

Sayeed slowly stepped inside, allowing the tent flap to fall closed behind him. "Where are you going?"

She grabbed the hilt of the letter opener off the desk, waved it in front of her. "Don't you dare come near me."

"Kathleen, what's going on?" He kept coming toward her as he spoke. He held his hand out. "Give me the letter opener, Kathleen."

Her heart raced. "I swear, I'll kill you, you bastard."

"Look, just put that down, will you, and tell me what's going on."

"Did you tell Bakkar you're going to kill my sister tonight or later out in the desert?"

He stalled, shock on his face. "You speak the language," he said very quietly in Arabic. "I should have guessed it from your diary, seen it as a possibility."

"Back away from the entrance," she replied in the dialect.

He took a step closer, blocking her exit. "Kathleen, don't do this—"

"I mean it." Her hands started trembling. "I will kill you."

He held up both hands. "Look, I won't hurt you, Kathleen—I promise."

"Like you promised you had no idea where Jennie was before you slept with me!"

He had the audacity to look hurt, then anger growled into his features. "You wanted me, Kathleen. I tried to stop several times."

Tears began to roll down her cheeks. "I…I wanted something that was a lie… It…it's always like that. I am such a goddamn fool."

He reached for the letter opener in her hands, but she barreled at him with full force. The dull blade sank into his side. He froze in shock, glanced down at the blade sticking out of him.

Horror gushed through Kathleen.

She hesitated, then she turned and fled out of the tent into the dark dawn, running as fast as she could to where she'd seen the horses corralled.

Chapter 8

Sayeed doubled over in pain. Slowly, he slid the blade out of his flesh. He lifted his robes as he stumbled over to the first aid kit, quickly stanching the blood and checking out the damage. The blade hadn't gone deep, thank God. It had deflected off his leather belt, traveling along the outer edge of his waist, seemingly missing any major organ or arteries. But it made for a lot of blood. He plugged the wound with wadding from the first aid kit and plastered adhesive tape tightly over the top. He took a handgun from the drawer on his desk, a spare magazine, and then he slipped out into the darkness. He had to find Kathleen fast, before someone else did, or she was dead.

Kathleen rode quietly along the shadowed cliff edges, under rocks that jutted out above her head. Dawn had not yet broken, but the sky had lightened just enough for her to see where she was going—she might manage to avoid the sentries she'd spotted along the cliff face when Sayeed brought her through the canyon the first time.

She tried to remember where she'd first seen the trail zigzagging up to the castle ruins on the ridge. Her intention was to go up there, try to find Jennie. She didn't know what else to do. She couldn't ride out into the desert. She had no water, no direction—she'd die before she managed to find help or alert anyone. So she focused on trying to get to her sister. It's all she could think to do right now.

Scanning the ground with his flashlight, Sayeed saw Kathleen's footprints heading from his tent toward the stables. He switched off his light and ran in a crouch toward the horses.

There was a quiet air of industry in the rest of the compound—instructions had been given to decamp and be cleared out by tomorrow morning. By then, the biological attack was supposed to be well under way, and the Moors were going to lay low in respective hiding places for several months. This was good. In the unusual flurry of early morning activity Sayeed had a fair chance of bringing Kathleen back into camp unnoticed. But once the sun came up, all bets were off.

When he reached the stables, Sayeed panned his light over the horses. They were edgy, one whinnying. The sand outside the gate had been recently disturbed.

He opened the gate, quietly entered the corral and selected his favorite gelding. Once he'd led his horse outside the gate, Sayeed mounted and headed at a clip for the canyon. He'd seen the way Kathleen had been looking up at the castle ruins and the switchback trail when he'd first brought her through the canyon. He was betting she'd go there if she'd overheard everything said outside his tent.

As he rode, his admiration for Kathleen deepened. She was

not trained, not equipped for this. Yet, she'd played him. She'd had the guts to stab him and get away. But if those sentries didn't kill her now, the Sahara certainly would.

Dawn bled violent pinks and purples into the sky. With relief Kathleen could see the twisting trail up to the castle ruins ahead. She'd made it through the canyon and past the sentries without being spotted before the sun came over the ridge.

She kicked her horse into a gallop, aiming for the trail.

Then suddenly she heard the sound of hooves bearing down behind her. Shock smashed through her. She rode harder but not well—bouncing about all over the horse. Kathleen became so focused on just holding on, staying alive, not falling, that she didn't even dare look behind her.

The hooves sounded louder, faster, closing in.

Terror clawed through her. The sky grew brighter, the air hotter. She rode harder, sweat dripping down between her breasts and under her turban.

The hooves were right behind her now. Her horse foamed at the mouth, then it stumbled. She went over its head, landing hard on the sand.

Her pursuer swung off his horse and came down right on top of her. She tried to get up, run. But he wrestled her back into the sand, her turban coming off in the process, grains of sand grinding into the side of her face as he pressed her down.

She tried to scream, but he killed the sound by clamping his hand hard over her mouth.

His body was big, hard. Hot. She felt his heart beat against her rib cage. The sound of her own blood beat a loud tattoo in her eardrums. Sand burned her eyes, gritted in her teeth, got up her nose.

"Quiet," he hissed in her ear.

Sayeed.

"Do not scream, or they will come and kill you, do you understand this?" He spoke in Arabic.

She nodded, tears of pain mixing with hard grains of sand, rocks pressing into her side.

Sayeed eased off her a little and removed his hand from her mouth. Her face was bloodless, her eyes hostile. She was shaking like a leaf. Sand covered her face, her clothes.

But she didn't try to run, and he helped her up into a sitting position. Her attention shot straight to his waist, where she'd stabbed him, then back to his face. He knew he looked like crap. He knew he'd lost a fair bit of blood in the exertion of the chase. But it was not remorse he read in her eyes—it was pure hatred.

"You bastard!" she spat at him. "You knew where Jennie was all the time. You made me believe in you—you *promised* me."

"Kathleen, I know it looks bad, but you've got to believe me, I'm on your side."

"You're a terrorist!"

The sun's rays hit the opposite cliff. The clock was ticking. He had to get back.

"Kathleen, please, just listen to me—"

"Why should I?" she said, her eyes red, burning. "You used me, Sayeed. You...you had sex with me when you were intending to kill my sister. You..." Her voice hitched. She struggled for focus. "You knew how very deeply important Jennie is to me, and...and I can't believe I'm so goddamn stupid." She broke down, exhausted, crying into her hands.

He placed his hand on her shoulder, but she jerked away, getting to her feet, staggering through soft sand toward the cliff where the switchback trail started.

"Kathleen!"

She kept walking. He lunged up and grabbed her arm.

She spun around, furiously swinging her fist at his face. He gripped her wrist, halting her. Time was running out, and Sayeed spoke fast, knowing his only way forward was to regain a measure of her trust and get her back to camp, stat. But he was also sworn to absolute secrecy—the stakes of this mission were monumental. An army waited over the border for his signal. Everything hinged on him maintaining his cover. But he had to do it—he had to tell her everything and trust her with his secret if he wanted her trust in return.

"I'm not a terrorist, Kathleen—I'm not one of those men. My name is not Sayeed Ali."

She stilled.

"I'm Rashid Al Barrah. I'm working undercover for the CIA."

"I…don't believe you."

"Come over here, out of the wind." Reluctantly, she allowed him to lead her into the lee of a large dune. She looked up at the shimmering ruins along the cliff as she sat down, the sun's morning rays hitting the crumbling red stone turrets.

He couldn't begin to imagine what Kathleen felt in discovering her sister was being held up there, in the bowels of the ancient castle, being forced to do terrible things. Rashid—for he could not think of himself as Sayeed right now—inhaled deeply, struggling with his own decision to bring her into the loop. If his cover was blown and she was captured, this information could hurt her. She'd be tortured.

Hell, if she was captured, she was going to die anyway, and these men were not going to be nice about it, no matter what she knew.

He had to tell her, *and* he had to keep her safe.

"I'm an FBI agent, Kathleen. Up until three years ago, I worked out of the Washington, D.C., field office—"

Her eyes flashed, and she glowered at him. "I don't believe you. I don't believe anything you say."

"Will you just hear me out?"

She glanced away.

He moistened his lips. "The CIA asked if I'd go undercover to help take down this terrorist cell. It's one of several cells under direct command of a man known only as The Moor. We don't know yet where he lives, or who he is. But one leader in each cell gets his orders directly from The Moor, and Bakkar is that man in this particular cell. And while infiltrating this cell over a period of over two years, I learned through Bakkar that The Moor is orchestrating a massive biological suicide attack on major U.S. cities and the cities of U.S. allies around the globe. The plan is to inject a genetically modified form of Ebola Botou into the blood of forty volunteers at 1900 hours tonight. Those infected volunteers will then fly to major airport hubs around the world, spreading the virulent disease as they go. And once they land, they will continue visiting major population centers and transport systems until they succumb to the virus and die." He checked his watch. He had to move faster.

"My instructions are to wait until they are injected," he said. "Until everyone is in one place, then I will sound the alarm that will precipitate an attack. Special ops forces will bomb the hell out of the lab within sixty minutes of me sounding the alarm, killing the virus and volunteers before they can become infectious. A simultaneous raid will take place on Bakkar's camp."

She stared at him. "Jennie—she's part of this?"

He nodded. "She was taken by the Maghreb Moors and was forced to continue the work started by a scientist who died on the job."

Kathleen went sheet white. "Why would the CIA pick an FBI agent for this? Why *you?*"

She still wasn't buying his story, and he couldn't blame her. Rashid was going to have to go deeper and get personal.

"Because I speak the local dialect fluently and am familiar with this region and the clan customs. In particular, I have specific insight into the minds of Bakkar and Marwan. I was born here, Kathleen. I share their blood."

"Al Barrah," she whispered. "You said Bakkar's name was Al Barrah."

"He's my father. He banished me from his home when I was eleven, and he doesn't yet know I am his son."

"Why did he banish you?"

Rashid looked up at the sky. The sun was beating down, temperatures rising. The volunteers would be arriving soon. And he didn't want to talk about his mother. Or his childhood. But he also needed to get Kathleen back to camp fast. "When I was eleven my uncle Marwan raped my mother," he said. "My father—Bakkar—was incensed, and he blamed her, not Marwan. He burned my mother's face with hot oil so no man would ever look at her again, then he banished her from his compound, sending her out in the desert to die. I fled after her, to help her. But first I cut my father's face with his own *jambiya*."

Kathleen stared at him, the image of Bakkar Al Barrah clawing back into her mind—the hideous scar across his face, the downturned eye. The genetic echoes in the features and builds of Marwan, Bakkar, Qasim. And yes, she could see those echoes now in Rashid.

"Did she survive? Did you manage to save your mother?"

"We walked and walked until we found a *wadi* where she collapsed. She'd developed an infection and gone blind. A small caravan of nomads found us. They had an old man with them who knew ancient medicine, herbs and things. He managed to halt my mother's infection with a thick salve that kept sand out and with herbs that brought her fever down. They transported her on camel and took us into Morocco."

Rashid paused. Memories twisted his features, rage, hurt, pain glimmering through his eyes.

"What happened then?" she said softly.

"An international women's rights organization learned of my mother's plight and found a benefactor who funded medical treatment and plastic surgery in the States. My mother got well again but was terribly scarred both physically and emotionally, and she never regained her sight. We did however gain a new home, a new country. I grew up on the East Coast, and after a presentation at my school, I decided I wanted to be an FBI agent. I followed that dream, Kathleen. Now, here I am. Back where it all started."

From the raw emotion in his eyes, Kathleen wanted to believe him. But she remained cautious. People could feign this stuff, especially terrorists and criminals. Then she remembered the tattoo. "Is it real—the tattoo? Are you all descended from the Sun Clan?"

Surprise showed in his face. "You know about the Sun Clan?"

"I'm an historian, Sayeed—"

"Rashid," he corrected gently. "My name is Rashid. And yes, the tattoo is real. Just like what we shared in bed was real, Kathleen," he said softly. "The man who lay with you was *me*. And when we get out of here, I want to see you again. I want to get to know you better."

She rubbed her face, hiding her emotion. "I don't know if I can believe you."

He touched her. "When we raided your camp, I couldn't let them kill you, Kathleen, even though I'd been instructed to allow some collateral damage if necessary. Saving you almost blew my cover, and if you don't come back to camp with me now, it *will* be blown. Your sister and thousands of others will end up dying."

"So the authorities knew—through you—that Jennie had been taken and was a part of this."

"Yes. But we couldn't pull her out earlier, not without alerting key players like Bakkar and Marwan and sending this all underground again. We had to wait until the last moment for maximum effect."

She swore. "So that's why I was stonewalled. Jennie's just a pawn. Collateral damage. Do you even plan to take her out before you bomb the hell out of that place up there?"

"I won't let her die."

"But you were going to?"

"Kathleen—"

She lurched to her feet, panic, distaste, raking through her.

He got up, grabbed both her wrists. "I said I won't let it happen. For you. I'm going to try and get *both* of you out of here, alive, understand?"

"How?"

"You heard that man outside the tent. Bakkar has ordered me to go up there and kill Jennie. It's a test, I'm sure. One of many. But it's going to work in our favor, Kathleen, because I persuaded Bakkar Jennie must live until the volunteers arrive at their destinations and there is proof the modified virus is airborne and working. This will enable me to take her out of the lab and get her into the desert before the raid. But you've got to help me. And you must also understand, and accept, the risks. We could all die."

"I…I'll do anything. Just tell me what."

"Okay, the only way up there is via mule right now. That's how I will go up tonight. And when we travel up there, we always take one of the young stable hands for the mules—I will try to disguise and pass you off as my stable hand. Bakkar said there will be a four-wheel-drive vehicle waiting up on the plateau, outside the castle, for me to use when I take Jennie from the lab to a designated holding place. It will be one of the vehicles that was used to transport some of the volunteers to the castle. It's fairly easy to drive to the castle from the north, if you know where you are going. And, Kathleen, if we are truly lucky, we will get out before the raid. But one little mistake, one wrong word, one glance at the wrong time—and we die. Can you accept this?"

Shock, fear, the enormity of what was happening, stole Kathleen's words. Rashid gently cupped the side of her face. "Kathleen, can you do this, for Jennie?"

She inhaled deeply, nodded. "I have to." She paused. "Rashid, thank you."

Hearing his real name uttered for the first time in almost three years did indescribable things to Rashid. He leaned forward and kissed her softly. He felt her tears against his cheek as he did. And he knew they were now a team. He also knew he'd found a woman he could love, forever if she'd let him. But first, he was going to have to earn that chance. He was going to have to make this raid happen and come out the other end, alive.

Rashid also knew he was not going to return for Bakkar and Marwan's lives. Not if it could cost him a chance at a future with Kathleen. His redemption would come from saving her life and her sister's now. He'd leave Bakkar and Marwan's fates to the special ops forces. He was going to leave the past, the ancient code of justice, here in the desert where the history belonged.

Chapter 9

Rashid took the cord from his robe and tightly bound Kathleen's wrists together in front of her. Doubt sifted into her eyes.

"Trust me, remember?" he said. "This is the only way we can realistically bring you back into camp. The sentries will be watching. Others will see us arriving. So we've got to hide in plain sight, okay? Can you follow my cues, Kathleen?"

She nodded.

He helped her onto her saddle and tied her wrists to the saddle horn.

"This is the story: You ran away from me. I chased you and am returning you to my quarters where you will do your wifely duty. I might have to be a little rough. Just remember, I'm doing what I can to save your life and Jennie's life."

She glanced up at the castle ruins on the cliff again, and her features turned resolute. "I understand."

He tied Kathleen's horse behind his, and they cantered

toward the canyon, Kathleen struggling to stay neatly on her mount. Rashid swallowed an urge to go easy on her. But anyone could be watching now—he had to maintain the facade.

They entered the canyon. He slowed their pace as he scanned the rock faces for signs of the sentries, making sure Kathleen's horse stayed behind him and that it looked obvious she was his prisoner. When he saw the first sentry step out of hiding, Rashid raised his hand in salute.

The man hesitated, then waved them on.

Rashid kicked up the pace and when they reached camp, he barreled into the enclosure at a full gallop with Kathleen grasping the saddle horn for dear life. Rashid's heart sank as he saw Qasim near the stables.

Rashid rode right up to his tent and dismounted, but Qasim came hurrying over. "What are you doing, Sayeed?" he demanded, suspicion darkening his eyes. "Where have you been?"

"The bitch stabbed me and escaped." Rashid showed his bloodied robes. "I went to get her back."

Qasim stared at the blood, then Rashid's face. Then he threw back his head and laughed. "Ha, you were not good enough in bed for her!"

"Get out of my way!" Rashid pushed Qasim aside and started cutting through the rope that bound Kathleen's wrists to the saddle. She looked rightfully and realistically terrified.

He dragged her down from the horse, and she fell hard to the ground. Rashid's chest tightened with compassion. But he pushed her with his boot. "Get up!" he barked in English. "Get up and get into my tent!"

She struggled to her feet and stumbled into his quarters.

As Rashid drew the tent flap down, he heard murmurs and more laughter outside. His heart raced. His body was drenched with sweat. "I think we made it," he whispered. "Did I hurt you?"

She shook her head, and he untied her wrists.

"What about you? Did I hurt you badly with the letter opener?"

"It's a surface gouge—just bled a lot."

"Can I look at it?"

"There's no time."

"Then make time," she said, forcing a smile. "I really can't afford to lose you now, Rashid." Her gaze met his, and Rashid knew they really were a team now.

He only hoped they might live long enough to try and stay that way.

Kathleen dressed the wound she'd given him. And as she tended to him, her emotions were overpowering—a mix of deep kinship, affection, admiration. She thought of what he'd said about making love to her and seeing her once this was over. She told herself it was the stress, the adrenaline, talking. She needed to stay focused on the present, for Jennie.

Once she'd plastered more adhesive tape tightly over the cut, Rashid sat her down and began to smear brown boot polish onto her face. He then wound a turban carefully around her head leaving a very thin slit for her eyes. "It'll be getting dark when we go up," he said. "If you keep your head down and keep quiet this might work."

He began smearing polish on the backs of her hands and wrists.

"How will we see where we're going in the dark?"

"There'll be a moon tonight, stars, and we will have head-lamps."

She nodded. He went to his desk, rummaged under some papers and removed a handgun. "Ever used one of these?"

"No."

"I hope you don't have to, but I want you to carry it just in case something happens to me." He showed her how to reload it and where the safety was. Then he gave her a holster to tuck under the fabric at her waist.

"Before we leave, I'll tell Bakkar that I've asked one of his men to guard you in my quarters."

"What if he comes looking?"

"I suspect he will. He'll want to kill you while I am gone, Kathleen. Remember, he thinks I am heading into the desert with Jennie to wait for news of the volunteers' success. Theoretically, you will have been abandoned, and he's going to want to tie up loose ends before they break camp and flee."

"And when he finds I'm not here?"

"Best-case scenario, he'll think you got away. He won't know any different until this is over."

"What if he radios up to the castle or something?"

"No radio communication is allowed from this camp. They don't want to be picked up by scanners. We've strictly used human messengers." Rashid stepped back and examined his handiwork. Then he smiled. "I think you'll pass. You ready for this?"

"Let's do it."

He suddenly hugged her, just holding her tight for several beats, his reason for wanting to protect now fiercely personal—he wanted her in his future.

"Rashid, thank you," she whispered. And when she pulled away, he saw tears in her eyes.

Chapter 10

Kathleen stood in the corner of a dark stone room as she watched the suicide volunteers emerging from the level-four biohazard protection area that had been built into the dungeons of the ancient castle. The men were coming through a door into another containment area that was behind a pane of glass. Rashid stood near, but not too close.

Then as the fortieth volunteer entered the containment area, Kathleen caught sight of Jennie coming through the door behind him.

Shock jolted through her.

Jennie was alive!

But she looked terrible—reed thin, pale, her eyes like dark holes. Immobilized with emotion, Kathleen stared at her sister, every molecule in her body screaming to bash through the glass, go help Jennie.

"Get your head down!" Rashid hissed quietly at her.

Kathleen lowered her head but kept Jennie fixed in her

peripheral vision. Rashid had told her that once Jennie had injected the volunteers with the virus, they'd be brought up to this staging area. From here, they would leave for their destinations around the world.

The men would become contagious within fourteen hours but not show real symptoms for another twenty-one days. From then, death would be fast and terrible.

Kathleen saw Rashid reaching into the folds of his robe. She knew he was about to press the satellite alarm now that he'd seen all forty volunteers emerge.

Her heart kicked—they now had exactly sixty minutes to get out of the castle and race into the desert. And once they were out in the desert, when Rashid pressed the button a second time, a military chopper would fly toward the GPS coordinates being submitted by his beacon. The chopper would land and evacuate them as long as it was safe.

Having pressed the alarm, Rashid started to move to the locked door. On the other side of the glass, a guard also moved toward the door. But before the guard could unlock it, one of the volunteers began to stagger. Blood poured suddenly from his mouth, and his eyes turned red from bursting veins.

The guards spun around and stared in shock at the man. Another one of the volunteers also started to bleed and slumped to the ground. Then a few more. Panic hit. Men started running. And Kathleen saw Jennie in the corner, reaching for the dagger of one of the men who'd collapsed.

Terror gripped Kathleen's chest. "I know what she's done!" she whispered to Rashid. "She's killing them! She couldn't let it happen—" Suddenly Kathleen saw what her sister was doing with the dagger. Jennie had pulled up her sleeve and was holding her wrist out, putting the blade on it.

"She's going to kill herself!"

Rashid bashed on the locked door. The guards inside shook

their heads, terror in their eyes. Kathleen fumbled in her robes for the gun Rashid had given her. With shaking hands she aimed at the glass and pulled the trigger.

"No!" yelled Rashid.

But it was too late. The glass pane shattered, sliding to the stone floor with an explosive crash. And all hell broke loose as guards spun around and started shooting at Kathleen.

Rashid cursed and yanked out his weapon, returning fire as he shoved Kathleen to the ground. "Crawl out of here," he yelled. "Go to your right until you get to stairs. Then go down to the dungeons."

She hesitated. Bullets blew out pieces of rock above her head.

"Now!"

"What about Jennie!"

"I'll get her. Move. We have fifty-eight minutes!"

Kathleen crawled to the exit.

Rashid edged up to the blown-out window. One of the guards had opened the door, and others were now fleeing, panicked about infection from the bleeding and fallen volunteers. Jennie was lying in the corner, unconscious.

Rashid entered the room and climbed over the bodies toward her. Her wrist was bleeding, but she had not yet cut deep enough to do fatal damage. She must have been hit with flying debris when the glass exploded before she could kill herself.

He scooped her up in his arms. She was light as a bird. Carrying her, Rashid dashed out of the antechamber and ran into the dark, stone passage. Turning on his headlamp, he veered right, and ran for the steps that led into the dungeon.

He could hear men screaming and footsteps on stone.

* * *

"Over here!" he heard Kathleen whisper from a small alcove on the stairs.

"Oh, God," she said as he laid Jennie on the stone. "Is she okay?"

"She's unconscious." Under the light of his headlamp, Rashid ripped cloth from his robe and tightly bound Jennie's cut wrist. Then he gathered her into his arms again. "There's a way out of here, a tunnel, but first we have to go down. And the route might be blocked, and if it is, we will not make it out alive. You okay with that?"

She nodded fast.

He led the way, carrying Jennie.

They had maybe forty minutes left. Rashid wasn't sure they'd reach the tunnel in time. He'd scoped it out months ago and was unsure if it had been sealed up in the interim.

"What about those volunteers?" Kathleen asked, running behind him, breathless. "Are they infected? Did I release the virus?"

"Just shut up and run, and next time, follow my goddamn orders!"

Rashid had no idea what Jennie had done to the virus or if those fleeing guards would spread it. Or if he and Kathleen would die from exposure to it. And Jennie sure wasn't in a position to tell them.

The tunnel was still accessible, but two wrong turns down dead ends had left Rashid and Kathleen exactly two minutes and twenty seconds to reach the Jeep that Bakkar said would be waiting outside.

Rashid's chest burned as he raced out of the tunnel toward the vehicle. They were lucky it was still where Bakkar said it would be, that one of the fleeing guards hadn't found it.

Tossing the unconscious Jennie into the back, Rashid leaped into the driver's seat and started the engine.

Kathleen scrambled into the back with her sister. She held Jennie close as Rashid spun the Jeep around in sand and fishtailed over the plateau toward the west.

Kathleen heard jets.

Then she felt the jolt of shock waves as explosions lit the sky.

She held Jennie's head in her lap and prayed.

Rashid continued driving for what seemed like hours. Kathleen wished there was water for her sister. The sun came up, and heat rippled once more through a bleak Sahara landscape.

Finally, Rashid pulled up behind a rock formation. His features were tight. He hadn't said a word to her since he'd chided her for shooting the glass.

He reached for his satellite beacon and pressed the button a second time. Then he examined Jennie.

"Do you think the virus got out?" Kathleen said again.

He didn't answer. He got out of the Jeep and walked into the sand.

Kathleen could hear thudding in the air. The helicopter materialized out of shimmering sky to the northwest. Never had anything looked or sounded more welcome.

Rashid waved his arm in a slow arc.

The chopper aimed for him.

When it set down, the pilot didn't switch off the bird. He kept the rotors turning. He wore a hazmat suit, as did his passenger. The passenger—a special ops soldier, Kathleen guessed—helped Rashid lift Jennie into the craft. He then helped her up and buckled her in. Rashid hopped out of the chopper and gave a signal.

The helo started to rise.

"Why are we leaving him?"

No one replied. Rashid stood below, getting smaller as they climbed rapidly into the air. Kathleen pressed her hand to the glass, desperate, watching him turn into a tiny speck of brown in a sea of yellow sand. Tears streamed down her face as he disappeared into the landscape

She stroked Jennie's forehead as they flew. "Please, stay with me, Jenn," she whispered. "Don't you dare go dying on me now—not aftner all this."

Chapter 11

Three months later

After an intensive debriefing in Washington, D.C., Kathleen was finally back at work in Seattle. It was autumn and the gray rains and cool mists of the Pacific Northwest had socked in, bringing the sky low and her mood even lower.

Being at the airport to say goodbye to Jennie didn't help.

Her sister had come to stay with her in Seattle for a while after her own extensive debriefing and therapy, but now Jennie felt ready to return east and go back to her work at the university.

The two sisters were sharing lunch at a small table beside the large rain-flecked windows as they watched the planes coming and going through the mist, waiting for Jennie's boarding call.

Jennie had regained some of the weight she'd lost, and

although she appeared aged, she was looking as good as might be expected. For that, Kathleen was immensely grateful.

After the helicopter evacuation in the Maghreb, her sister had been treated immediately at a military base, then flown to a hospital in Germany where she'd come out of her coma. Jennie had then managed to tell the U.S. authorities she had not injected the men with a contagious form of Ebola Botou. Instead, she'd modified the virus in a way that it would kill the men almost immediately without spreading. She'd destroyed the earlier version she'd been forced to test on a first batch of volunteers, secretly replacing it with her later version. Jennie had planned to kill the volunteers, then kill herself, rather than be responsible for unleashing a plague on the world.

For that, she should have become an instant hero. Instead, the entire event had been kept under the radar of the press for ongoing security reasons.

"You sure you're ready to go back to work, Jenn?" Kathleen said, pushing her salad around with her fork, not terribly hungry.

Jennie smiled and placed her hand over Kathleen's. "I couldn't be more ready—I need to go back, to focus forward, put this whole thing behind me."

Emotion swelled behind Kathleen's eyes and she nodded. "I'll miss you."

"Why don't you come back east with me, Kathleen?" Jennie said. "Maybe the change—a new job, a fresh place—would be good."

"It would feel too close to him."

"Rashid?"

Kathleen nodded, pushing her plate to one side.

"He never returned your calls?"

"I really don't want to speak about it, Jenn—"

"You must."

"Why? What difference will it make? I was an idiot to have even dared dream it could work with him."

"Maybe there's a reason he hasn't called."

"Yeah, like he thinks I'm a freak. I know he's back stateside—the Washington field office told me that. I called his work several times and each time someone told me he was busy or unavailable. I should've just taken the hint. But I found a home number for him and called many times, and only ever got voice mail."

"You leave messages?"

Kathleen snorted. "Plenty. I finally stopped leaving them, but sometimes I just called…you know, to hear his voice. Sometimes I wonder if I hadn't shot the glass, if I'd obeyed his orders, if things might be different."

"It saved my life, your disobeying his orders."

Kathleen nodded, bit her lip, dug into her purse for a tissue. She blew her nose.

"I'm an ass, Jenn. We were both pawns. My mistake was falling for it, for him." She straightened her shoulders. "I'm going to move on now."

Jennie's gaze held hers, and Kathleen could see the doubt in her sister's eyes. But before she could say anything else, they heard Jennie's boarding call.

"That's for me," Jennie said, getting up.

Tension kicked into Kathleen. She stood up, hugged her sister tight. "I'm going to miss you like hell."

"I love you, kiddo," Jennie said. "Thank you. Thank you for coming for me. Thank you for not giving up. Thank you for believing you could do this."

Tears swelled into Kathleen's eyes and she was unable to speak. She just nodded, hugging her sister one more time before stepping back to watch Jennie walk away. And she'd never felt more lost and lonely in her life.

The Sahara had changed her, opened her, and she no longer

felt as if she fit into her own life. Kathleen wondered if she'd ever be happy at home again. Even the job she'd once loved now felt dissatisfying, the library walls too close, everything too dark. Maybe Jennie was right, maybe she did need to move away, think about starting over somewhere fresh.

Kathleen left the airport and, instead of returning to work, she called and told her colleagues she wouldn't be coming back in today. Instead, she drove down to the sea wall. A walk might clear her mind.

It was late Friday afternoon and the sky was turning a dark battleship-gray. The ocean was stormy. A fine mist dampened her skin and hair and she could feel the first drops of rain beginning to come down. A ship's foghorn sounded out in the mist. Kathleen pulled her coat closer, thinking of sun, heat. The desert. Big skies.

Of him.

Story of her life, she thought, stupid dreams. Idealistic notions. Romantic ideas that could never live up to reality.

As she neared the end of the wall, a dark figure emerged from thick mist. Kathleen's pulse quickened. It was desolate here. Getting late and dark. She began to turn around. But something about the shape made her stand still.

The man came closer and her heart began to race with a jolt of familiarity. He walked just like Rashid. He was the same height.

Frozen by memories, translating them into this form, she stood mesmerized. The man came closer, his dark black coat flapping about his calves in the wind. Head bare. Making straight for her.

And shock rippled through her.

It was him—Rashid Al Barrah—walking out of the mist like a dream.

Her throat closed in on itself. Her heart skipped and

tammered. Kathleen didn't dare breathe lest she shatter the ision she seemed to have conjured out of the mist.

But it wasn't a vision. He was real. And she heard his oice—his rich, deep, rolling baritone. "Kathleen."

She opened her mouth, but couldn't speak. He touched er.

"Kathleen, are you all right?"

She shook her head, tears beginning to spill from her yes.

He took her into his arms, just holding for an eternity. They told me at your work I'd find you down here," he vhispered against her ear.

Then he pulled back, looked deep into her eyes. "I'm so orry," he said. "After you left, I was sent right back out into he field. They had a lead on the identity of The Moor, and hey needed me. We got him, Kathleen. We got The Moor. Ie's an old man, but a very dangerous one."

"Who is he?"

"Bakkar and Marwan's father."

"Your grandfather," she whispered.

"My grandfather."

"What about Bakkar and Marwan, Qasim…everyone lse?"

"Marwan and Qasim were killed in the raid. Bakkar is in ustody. He started talking when he learned who I was. That's ow we got our break on The Moor."

"I'm pleased, Rashid. I…I missed you. I left messages—" he felt stupid. Of course he knew she'd plugged his machine p with voice mail.

He cupped her face. "I heard your messages."

"Yeah. Sorry. I should—"

"Kathleen, I heard them only yesterday. I just got back, and learned that because of the highly sensitive nature of what I

was doing, they'd made a decision not to tell you where I was
I'd asked them to let you know, Kathleen."

"I thought…" Tears filled her eyes.

"I'm so sorry." He lifted her face to the mist, his black eye
crackling with ferocity. And he kissed her hard. Heat sparked
through her body, her knees going weak.

"I've come home, Kathleen," he murmured against her lips
"I want to show you your dream *can* come true, that I war
the very same things you do. If you'll let me."

And Kathleen's world spun. Her girlhood dreams of finding
her own dashing desert prince, her knight in shining armor
really had come true.

"Will you let me, Kathleen?"

She nodded, laughing and crying. Then she wrapped her
arms tight around him and stood on tiptoe, kissing her own
desert knight. And suddenly the mist and rain were no longer
cold, and her world felt bright.

* * * * *

COMING NEXT MONTH

Available June 28, 2011

#1663 JUST A COWBOY
Conard County: The Next Generation
Rachel Lee

#1664 PRIVATE JUSTICE
The Kelley Legacy
Marie Ferrarella

#1665 SOLDIER'S LAST STAND
H.O.T. Watch
Cindy Dees

#1666 SWORN TO PROTECT
Native Country
Kimberly Van Meter

You can find more information on upcoming
Harlequin® titles, free excerpts and more at
www.HarlequinInsideRomance.com.

REQUEST YOUR FREE BOOKS!
2 FREE NOVELS PLUS 2 FREE GIFTS!

◊ Harlequin®

ROMANTIC
SUSPENSE

Sparked by Danger, Fueled by Passion.

YES! Please send me 2 FREE Harlequin® Romantic Suspense novels and my 2 FREE gifts (gifts are worth about $10). After receiving them, if I don't wish to receive any more books, I can return the shipping statement marked "cancel." If I don't cancel, I will receive 4 brand-new novels every month and be billed just $4.24 per book in the U.S. or $4.99 per book in Canada. That's a saving of at least 15% off the cover price! It's quite a bargain! Shipping and handling is just 50¢ per book in the U.S. and 75¢ per book in Canada.* I understand that accepting the 2 free books and gifts places me under no obligation to buy anything. I can always return a shipment and cancel at any time. Even if I never buy another book, the two free books and gifts are mine to keep forever.

240/340 SDN FC95

Name	(PLEASE PRINT)

Address	Apt. #

City	State/Prov.	Zip/Postal Code

Signature (if under 18, a parent or guardian must sign)

Mail to the **Reader Service:**
IN U.S.A.: P.O. Box 1867, Buffalo, NY 14240-1867
IN CANADA: P.O. Box 609, Fort Erie, Ontario L2A 5X3

Not valid for current subscribers to Harlequin Romantic Suspense books.

Want to try two free books from another line?
Call 1-800-873-8635 or visit www.ReaderService.com.

* Terms and prices subject to change without notice. Prices do not include applicable taxes. Sales tax applicable in N.Y. Canadian residents will be charged applicable taxes. Offer not valid in Quebec. This offer is limited to one order per household. All orders subject to credit approval. Credit or debit balances in a customer's account(s) may be offset by any other outstanding balance owed by or to the customer. Please allow 4 to 6 weeks for delivery. Offer available while quantities last.

Your Privacy—The Reader Service is committed to protecting your privacy. Our Privacy Policy is available online at www.ReaderService.com or upon request from the Reader Service.

We make a portion of our mailing list available to reputable third parties that offer products we believe may interest you. If you prefer that we not exchange your name with third parties, or if you wish to clarify or modify your communication preferences, please visit us at www.ReaderService.com/consumerchoice or write to us at Reader Service Preference Service, P.O. Box 9062, Buffalo, NY 14269. Include your complete name and address.

HRS11

USA TODAY *bestselling author B.J. Daniels
takes you on a trip to Whitehorse, Montana,
and the Chisholm Cattle Company.*

RUSTLED

Available July 2011 from Harlequin Intrigue.

As the dust settled, Dawson got his first good look at the rustler. A pair of big Montana sky-blue eyes glared up at him from a face framed by blond curls.

A woman rustler?

"You have to let me go," she hollered as the roar of the stampeding cattle died off in the distance.

"So you can finish stealing my cattle? I don't think so." Dawson jerked the woman to her feet.

She reached for the gun strapped to her hip hidden under her long barn jacket.

He grabbed the weapon before she could, his eyes narrowing as he assessed her. "How many others are there?" he demanded, grabbing a fistful of her jacket. "I think you'd better start talking before I tear into you."

She tried to fight him off, but he was on to her tricks and pinned her to the ground. He was suddenly aware of the soft curves beneath the jean jacket she wore under her coat.

"You have to listen to me." She ground out the words from between her gritted teeth. "You have to let me go. If you don't they will come back for me and they will kill you. There are too many of them for you to fight off alone. You won't stand a chance and I don't want your blood on my hands."

"I'm touched by your concern for me. Especially after you just tried to pull a gun on me."

"I wasn't going to shoot you."

Dawson hauled her to her feet and walked her the rest of the way to his horse. Reaching into his saddlebag, he pulled out a length of rope.

"You can't tie me up."

He pulled her hands behind her back and began to tie her wrists together.

"If you let me go, I can keep them from coming back," she said. "You have my word." She let out an unladylike curse. "I'm just trying to save your sorry neck."

"And I'm just going after my cattle."

"Don't you mean your boss's cattle?"

"Those cattle are mine."

"*You're* a Chisholm?"

"Dawson Chisholm. And you are…?"

"Everyone calls me Jinx."

He chuckled. "I can see why."

Bronco busting, falling in love…it's all in a day's work. Look for the rest of their story in

RUSTLED

Available July 2011 from Harlequin Intrigue wherever books are sold.